Deadly Designs

Kathryn Keller

DEADLY DESIGNS

Kathryn Keller

Writers Club Press
New York Lincoln Shanghai

Deadly Designs

All Rights Reserved © 2003 by Kathryn Keller

No part of this book may be reproduced or transmitted in any form or by any means, graphic, electronic, or mechanical, including photocopying, recording, taping, or by any information storage retrieval system, without the written permission of the publisher.

Writers Club Press
an imprint of iUniverse, Inc.

For information address:
iUniverse, Inc.
2021 Pine Lake Road, Suite 100
Lincoln, NE 68512
www.iuniverse.com

ISBN: 0-595-26983-4 (pbk)
ISBN: 0-595-74644-6 (cloth)

Printed in the United States of America

Chapter 1

The hair prickling on the nape of her neck, she spun around at the sound of footfalls shuffling in the sand behind her. Scattered clouds partially obliterated the moon's pale lunar light, deepening the darkness around her.

A myriad of noises filtered through the windless night air. The gurgling of the waves along the shore. The muffled hoot of a horned owl from the black deepness of the nearby woods. The sudden, almost unearthly fluttering of its wings as it left its perch, undoubtedly startled too, by the sound of the footsteps, or to swoop down on an unsuspecting prey. Then moving toward her, she saw a large, grotesque creature outlined in the moonlight. It was huge and towering and clothed in black. In the depths of the night, its face was a cadaverous blur beneath a dark, narrow brimmed cap.

Her knees locked.

Paralyzed, she stared at the dark form confronting her as if it were a creature in a horrible nightmare. The stench of fear pushed itself into her nostrils and flooded the spaces in her mind.

A scream rose in her throat and froze there.

In that moment, in spite of the fear that gripped her, she realized that the shape confronting her was not a Loch Ness monster that had emerged from the depths of the lake, but a large man. She began to run; her bare feet sank into the loose sand, slowing her progress. The tennis shoes she was carrying in her hand slipped from her grasp. The sweater she had draped over her shoulders against the evening chill fell away.

Swifter now and to the left, the footsteps sounded behind her.

Her throat was tight with fear; she could barely breathe.

Praying it would deter her pursuer, she switched directions and fled into the water. It wrapped around her legs, tugged at them with swirling tentacles as she floundered through it.

Then the menacing figure was upon her. Huge fingers fastened around her throat, turning the scream that rose there into a harsh gurgle. She thrashed wildly, churning, roiling the water around them. As he bore her back, her gaze was forced skyward, making it impossible to catch a closer glimpse of his shadowy face. All she saw was his massive outline looming above her.

Dark. Deadly. Powerful.

His voice was a deep growl. "Mess with me, Bitch, and you'll pay."

As the pressure of his grip intensified on her throat, she fought for breath to fill her air-starved lungs. She was scarcely conscious of the pain brought about by the suffocating fingers biting into her flesh.

The scarf she had tied around her hair slipped off her head and down around her neck. Miraculously until now, the scarf had remained in place. Freed of their bonds, strands of wet hair fell across her forehead and into her eyes, blinding her. Clawing out in desperation, she tried to wipe the hair out of her eyes. Then, unexpectedly, the deadly grip loosened on her throat. She fell backward. Water splashed in her face, filling her mouth and nostrils. She choked, gasped for air.

Stepping back, the hulking figure waded toward the shore, a small wake trailing after him. Seconds later, he was swallowed up by the oily blackness of the night.

Gasping, flailing the water around her, she regained her balance. Legs faltering and feet dragging, she staggered toward the house. The roaring in her ears made it impossible to determine if her assailant was behind her again, following her. Small pieces of stone embedded in the cement steps that led onto the lawn bit into the soles of her bare feet as she stumbled upward, hands grasping the metal railing.

Then she was across the patio and into the safety of the house. Her breathing ragged and her heart thundering against her ribs, she pulled the patio door shut and locked it. Checked it twice to make certain it was secure.

Expecting to be back shortly when she'd left for a stroll along the beach an hour or so ago, she hadn't switched off the living room lights. Crossing the carpet to the desk in the corner, she yanked open the drawer and groped inside.

Be there! Please be there! she prayed.

When her fingers touched cold steel, her gratitude was so intense she grabbed onto the edge of the desk to keep from fainting. Her hands shaking so badly she could barely hold onto the gun, she lifted it from the drawer.

She had never fired a weapon. Never killed a living thing larger than a spider. The thought of killing another human being filled her with revulsion. But hysteria and a primitive instinct for survival, she knew, could change all that. One hand still holding onto the desk for support, she held her breath and listened, senses tuned for the slightest threatening sound.

The ticking of the clock on the kitchen wall hammered in her ears.

Nothing else.

Lifting the phone atop the desk, she dialed 911. After reporting the assault, fingers trembling, she picked up the gun again. Seized with a heart-chilling sense that she was experiencing a horrific nightmare, she switched off the table lamps. The room plunged into darkness.

Groping for the chair alongside her, she eased herself onto it. Her hair was plastered to her head like a skullcap, and her wet clothing clung to her trembling body. Gripping the gun with both hands, she aimed it toward the patio door.

If anyone came through it, she was ready.

The humidity was almost a physical presence as it swept through the open window of Susan Edward's' blue Skyhawk. As it brushed against her cheeks with its hot breath, she reached up and wiped away the strand of short, brown hair that clung to her cheek.

Alongside the highway on Lake Sally, a sailboat with an orange spinnaker cut the lazy blue sky. The fragrance of pine resin and the smell of lake water evoked childhood memories, few of them happy. Paralleling the roadway, a train raced along the tracks, its wheels churning furiously, its whistle splitting the air. Many times, as a child, she had wished she were on a train, speeding away from this town. Away from the heartbreak and pain she'd had to endure.

Just ahead, a green and white sign announced the presence of a Holiday Inn. Across the highway another sign greeted 'WELCOME TO LAKE CENTER, Population 10, 450.' Except for a few changes, everything looked the same as it had when she had been here for her brother-in-law's funeral a little over a year ago. Plush. Green. Peaceful. Yet a sense of premonition preyed on the fringes of her mind.

"There's somethin' mighty strange goin' on with your sister."

The words had echoed over and over in Susan's mind ever since she received her uncle's disturbing phone call four days ago. For three hundred miles, all the way from her home in St. Paul, her head was filled with frightful connotations.

Susan's grip had tightened on the receiver at the sound of Harry's words. "What do you mean by something strange is going on?"

"I can't explain it. She's been hidin' out in the boonies ever since Brad was killed. She never comes into town. Rarely sees anyone."

"That certainly doesn't sound like Kim."

"I don't know what the hell's goin' on. I think…I think she might be havin' a breakdown." It was difficult for him to get out the words.

"A breakdown!" Susan repeated incredulously. "Kim never lets anything get to her—well, almost anything." Gregarious and outgoing, Kim challenged the world with shoulders squared and chin jutted out.

Dared it to defy her. Yet Harry seldom exaggerated or let his imagination run away with him.

"Somethin's not right." There was grimness, a hushed hesitancy in his voice. "Could you find time to come to Lake Center for a few days? Maybe you can figure out what's goin' on. You know how your sister feels about me. We've rubbed each other the wrong way since the day your Aunt Maggie and I took her in as an infant after your mother died. I love that girl as if she were my own flesh and blood, but she makes it damned hard sometimes."

Susan laughed knowingly. "I doubt if I'll have much influence over Kim. She has a mind of her own."

"Tell me about it! Your Aunt Maggie spoiled that girl rotten. It's too bad we didn't have kids of our own so Maggie could have spread her motherin' around. Your sister might have turned out the better for it." Harry paused reflectively. "Then there's that other thing that happened, too...."

Susan's stomach muscles tensed. "What other thing?"

"She didn't tell you?"

"I haven't heard from Kim in several months."

"She discovered someone tryin' to break into her house a while back. The guy roughed her up. Tried to rape her."

Susan's knuckles whitened as she clutched the receiver. "My God! Was she hurt?"

"She got a nasty cut on her head and her clothes were torn. Lucky for Kim the guy was scared off by a neighbor's dog that happened to wander into her yard."

A cold chill washed over Susan. Why hadn't her sister confided in her? Kim had no one else to turn to. They had lost both their parents—their mother from childbirth complications when Kim was born, and their father because of alcohol. Susan and Kim had been more like acquaintances than siblings while they were growing up. Susan had always yearned for a closer relationship with her sister, but it wasn't until a little over a year ago, after Kim's husband was killed, that they had become closer. Susan extended her sympathy to her sister and offered her support. And after Susan's divorce, Kim had done the same.

"My vacation is coming up next week," Susan told her uncle. "Mark wants me to come to Los Angeles for the two of us to try for a reconciliation, but I can come to Lake Center for a few days. Kim's the only family I have left. Mark will have to wait." Her ex-husband wouldn't like it, Susan was certain, but she couldn't turn her back on her sister.

Now, noticing that the gas gauge registered on empty, she pulled into the gas station on her left and eased up to a self-service pump. As she climbed out of her car and inserted the nozzle in the gas tank, a sheriff's patrol car turned off the street, its tires crunching on the concrete, and halted in front of the office.

An attendant with a two-day stubble on his face stepped out the door. "Afternoon, Reid. Out protectin' the public as usual?"

"Doin' my best," was the response from the uniformed deputy who climbed out of the patrol car.

Susan judged him to be at least six foot tall and in his late thirties or early forties. He wore no hat or cap. He had a mustache, and in need of a cut, thick dark hair sprinkled with touches of gray covered his head and grew down the nape of his neck. Broad jagged planes that left no room for soft handsomeness marked his high cheekbones and tightly fleshed skin.

The face was vaguely familiar. And the name.... The attendant had called him Reid. The deputy must be Reid Elison, Lake Center's former track and football star. Along with most of the other girls in town, she'd had a crush on him when she was a teenager. But he had dated only one girl. They had eventually married and moved away. Susan hadn't seen or heard about him in years.

"Have you found out who beat up the Hastings woman yet?" the attendant asked as he stood with his hands shoved into the pockets of his grease-stained coveralls. "My wife and I live in that area. She's been edgy since the incident happened. Keeps the doors locked all the time and has a baseball bat handy."

Susan stiffened, suddenly alert.

"Haven't found the guy yet," the deputy answered. "The description Ms Hastings gave fits half the guys in the county."

"Sounds frustratin'."

"Frustrating? It's strange as hell. Except for the bruise on her face and her torn shirt, there was no evidence to indicate that the assault ever happened. No witnesses. No scuff marks in the grass. And there should have been. The grass hadn't been cut in weeks. Although she reported the assault right away—or so she said—she acted as if she didn't want me to investigate."

"Maybe she knows who did it and is afraid to tell."

"Could be," the officer conceded as the two men walked into the office.

A chill swept over Susan. What had gone on at her sister's place?

After hanging up the hose and replacing the gas cap, she followed the two men into the station. Removing several bills from her wallet, she paid the attendant for the gas she had put in her car's tank, then turned to Reid Elison. "So you don't know what happened at the Hastings' place?"

His flint gray eyes swept over her, taking in her wrinkled shorts and the brief tank top that clung to her travel-weary torso. "We don't give out information about the cases we're working on."

What had he and the attendant been doing? They certainly hadn't been discussing the weather. "I'm Kim's sister, Susan Edwards."

"I still can't discuss the case with you, Ms Edwards. Police policy."

Determined not to be intimidated by his unyielding stance, Susan pulled back her shoulders. "I just recently learned what happened to Kim. I'm concerned about her."

Reid continued to study Susan, his penetrating gaze absorbing every detail of her appearance, as if he were collecting evidence from her softly rounded chin and short, brown hair. "You're Kim Hastings' sister? I don't remember you."

Susan lowered her gaze. Of course he didn't. A nondescript nobody during her teen years, she was seldom noticed by her peers. When informed that she and Kim were sisters, people found it difficult to comprehend.

Images of a good looking, sometimes mischievous teenager conflicted sharply with the unsmiling man confronting Susan now. Gone was his amicable, carefree persona. He was broader and heavier than he had been the last time she had seen him, right after his marriage to Linda Graham. The hair at his temples was frosted with gray, and deep lines were etched around his mouth and eyes. There was anger and something else—a sadness in this man.

"Your sister's injuries weren't serious," he assured her.

"Not this time," Susan challenged. "But somewhere out there a dangerous man is still on the loose. He could strike again."

"In spite of what you obviously believe, Ms Edwards, we're doing our best to find him." The steel in Reid Elison's voice underlined his statement distinctly.

"That's good to hear." Susan made no attempt to keep her lack of confidence in his efforts out of her voice. As the deputy drew in a sharp breath, she sensed the inner struggle he was waging with his temper.

His cold, gray eyes and tenacious demeanor sliced through her anger, tempering it slightly. She lowered her gaze. Stern words, disapproving looks—she was still vulnerable to both.

Chapter 2

▼

As Susan pulled her Skyhawk to a halt in front of the aging, white, two-story house where Harry lived, he hurried out, limping slightly from the arthritis that had plagued him for years. Wire-rimmed glasses perched precariously on the end of his Roman nose, and his pink scalp peeked through threads of thinning gray hair.

"Am I glad to see you!" A broad smile creased his weathered face into a mass of wrinkles. Along with the pleasure in his voice was a great sense of relief, as if a heavy weight had been lifted from his bony shoulders. "How was your drive up?"

"Long and hot." Susan felt the roughness of his lined face as she pressed her cheek against his and hugged him. "It's great to see you again."

A few minutes later they were seated across from each other in the living room sipping tall, refreshing glasses of iced tea.

"I prefer a can of cold beer myself, but Maggie wouldn't allow the stuff in the house," Harry said after taking a swallow from his glass and placing it on the end table beside him. "She was a wonderful woman. Kind. Caring. Compassionate. But she had a thing about alcohol…with good reason, as I'm sure you know all too well. I seldom keep booze in the fridge even now. Old habits die hard, I guess. But I have been known to participate in Happy Hour at Moe's bar now and then." His faded blue eyes danced mischievously. Then the smile slipped from his face. "I need a couple of bottles of courage before I can come back to this big, empty house."

"I know all about empty rooms and walls that stare back at you," Susan empathized.

As she glanced around, she saw that nothing had changed since her aunt had kept house. The same red and white checked curtains framed the kitchen windows. The same crocheted pillows huddled in the corners of the sofa. As she slid her hand across the sofa arm, the worn fabric scraped against her palm. A smile curved her lips as a picture of her aunt in her print cotton dress, an apron tied around her ample waist and an apple pie cooling on the cupboard, flashed into her mind.

"I have a cleanin' woman come in twice a month," Harry explained, noting Susan's glance. "I wash the dishes in between times—when there's nothin' left to eat on." He chuckled, the twinkle back in his eyes again.

"Are you still working at the newspaper office?" Susan asked.

"Still puttin' in my time. I do a feature story now and then. Most of the time I see to it that the others do things right. It's my privilege. I've been there for forty years."

"When are you going to retire and take it easy?"

"Retire? What would I do? Play poker and chase women? The poker I could handle, but I'm not sure about the women."

Susan laughed. "Come on. I'll bet they hang all over you."

Harry's pale blue eyes were dancing. "Like bees to clover blossoms." The smile faded from his wrinkled face. "I hope you can talk that sister of yours into movin' into town, at least for the summer. She won't listen to me. It's risky for her to be livin' out there alone. This is a tourist town. There's lots of kooks around the area this time of year." His concern for Kim's welfare appeared genuine, whether or not it was justified.

"I understand they haven't found the man who attacked Kim," Susan said.

Harry grunted. "Not as far as I know."

Anger rose to tinge Susan's voice as her thoughts returned to the scene that had taken place at the gas station, to Reid Elison's stern words and disapproving looks. "I don't suppose Lake Center's sheriffs' department is capable of solving anything very complicated."

"Old Tom Larson's still sheriff," Harry said. "He's gettin' up in years, but he's got a pretty good man in the department now. Name's Reid Elison. He's a local boy. Maybe you remember him."

"I ran into Mr. Elison at the Texaco station when I stopped for gas." His cold, arrogant manner had shattered the warm memories of the adolescent crush she'd had on him. "What's he doing back here?"

"His wife died a couple of years ago. He came back from Arizona where they'd been livin' since they got married."

"Linda's dead?" The loss of his wife could account for the shadows in his eyes, Susan conceded, her anger easing slightly. But it was no excuse for his abrupt manner.

She pushed aside the memory of the scenario at the gas station. "What did Kim tell you about the attack on her?"

"She didn't. I don't know a damned bit more than what was reported in the newspaper. She clams up whenever I ask her about it—not that I've had many opportunities to talk to her."

"Did you tell her I was coming?" Susan asked.

"I haven't seen Kim since I called you. She only answers the phone and her doorbell when she feels like it. When she finds out I asked you to come here and check on her, the shit will hit the fan."

Susan's brown eyes warmed in a conspiratorial smile. "I won't tell her if you don't."

"I don't intend to tell her. I value my life too much."

Susan laughed. Then, her smile fading, she checked her watch and saw that it was one thirty. "I suppose I'd better be going out to Kim's."

For some undefinable reason, she found herself holding back, apprehensive about going out to her sister's place for fear of what she would discover.

A half hour later, as Susan drove through the countryside, a smile tugged at her lips when she passed the small, gently waving fields of growing grain, the wooded groves, and meandering creeks that served as arteries between the many lakes. Somehow, the familiarity of the picturesque countryside, the quiet beauty and serenity, gave her a sense of security, of belonging, that she had never experienced while living in the city. She was still overwhelmed by St. Paul's hectic pace, its exhaust fumes, and never-ending noise. Yet there was nothing here for her except painful and unwanted memories.

Easing up on the accelerator, she turned off the highway and onto Ridge Wood Road, a narrow dirt road that wound around Long Lake and came out on the west side of Lake Center. Uncertain of the exact location of Kim's driveway since it had been some time since she'd been at Kim's place, Susan slowed her car to a crawl and began to check the names on the sparsely spaced mail boxes.

Then, noting a car behind her and not wanting to interfere with its progress, she pulled onto the side of the road and proceeded slowly. A quick glance in the rear view mirror revealed that the driver was signaling for a right turn. The car was an older model, slate blue in color. The driver, whose face was partially concealed by mirrored sunglasses, was quite possibly in his mid-thirties, with a short, light brown beard and wind-tossed hair.

Switching her attention back to the road, Susan spotted Kim's name on a mailbox a few yards ahead of her. She pulled down the blinker to indicate that she, too, was about to make a right turn. Inexplicably, the driver behind her released his signal and accelerated, his car's tires kicking up a spray of gravel as he sped past her. A frown creasing her forehead as he raced around a sharp corner and disappeared, she determined that, at the last moment, he must have realized he had made a mistake.

Several hundred yards long, Kim's driveway wound through a dense growth of trees with thick foliage and overhanging branches. Her rustic lake home was set against a green backdrop of towering elm, thick boughed spruce, and clusters of birch. Three or four inches high, the uncut grass and fuzz-capped dandelions on the lawn were as distracting as a wart on a beauty contestant's face.

The drapes were drawn across the large picture window that faced the driveway, giving the house a bleak, unoccupied look. Susan wondered if her sister was home. If not, where could she be? Harry had indicated that she'd become a recluse.

Standing on the steps, Susan pressed her finger on the doorbell. There was no response from within the house. She pushed the bell again.

She heard nothing except the rustle of the breeze in the leaves, and the chirping of birds as they fluttered through the trees, obviously disturbed by her sudden appearance.

When there was no response to another push on the doorbell, a prickly sensation tingled on the nape of her neck, and the pulse in her throat began to pound against her skin in hard, insistent little knocks.

Something had happened to her sister again—something terrible.

Chapter 3

Slowly, the door opened and Kim stood in the doorway.

Her brown eyes, which had always danced with a zest for life, were as bleak as a November landscape. Once a tumble of dazzling platinum threads, her long hair was limp and stringy. Her lips were drawn into a narrow, inexorable slit, as if she had forgotten how to smile.

"Sue!" she exclaimed, her jaw dropping in astonishment.

After embracing Susan, Kim chided, "Why didn't you tell me you were coming?"

Her feet were bare, and a short, terrycloth robe hung dejectedly from her bony shoulders. She was smiling, but Susan had sensed desperation in her sister's embrace. Kim's large, dark eyes were like black, smoldering coals. Compassion for her sister washing over her, Susan lifted her arms to pull Kim close again, to erase the hardness, the haunted look from her eyes. As if she sensed her thoughts, Kim drew back. Susan's arms fell to her side.

"I didn't call because I wanted to surprise you," she said in response to her sister's question. Her glance took in Kim's bathrobe and tousled hair. "Did you just get out of bed? It's almost three o'clock in the afternoon."

Kim shrugged with indifference. "What's to get up for?" She gestured for Susan to be seated on the sofa.

As she sat down, Susan's gaze slowly crept over Kim's thin figure. "You've lost weight since I last saw you."

"Maybe a few pounds."

Susan accepted that the botched break-in and attempted rape would make Kim more fearful, perhaps, more cautious. Although she had expected Kim to be depressed, perhaps uncertain, Susan hadn't expected to find her so devoid of caring, to have changed from an extrovert into a hermit. Could the loss of her husband be affecting Kim this much, or was something else going on with her?

Kim sat down on the arm of an overstuffed chair, one thin leg dangling over the side. "When did you get here? How long are you going to stay?" The words seemed to stumble over each other.

After Susan explained that she had arrived at Harry's place an hour or so ago, fidgeting with a strand of her pale, uncombed hair, Kim stood up from the arm of the chair. "Let's go into the kitchen. I'll make a pot of coffee."

When the coffee was ready, she filled two cups and edged herself onto a padded leather chair across the oval shaped, Formica-topped table from Susan. As Kim pushed back a pale strand of tangled hair from her face, Susan noticed a small scar on the side of her sister's brow.

"Why didn't you let me know about what happened to you?"

"What happened to me..." Kim's expression was blank. Her words hung suspended in the air.

"The break-in—the assault."

"Oh, that."

"Yes, that."

"I didn't want to worry you."

Puzzled by Kim's evasiveness, Susan urged, "Tell me about it now."

"I caught some creep trying to break into the house. When I confronted him, he shoved me around."

Susan shook her head in disbelief. "Harry said the guy tried to rape you, too."

Kim waved her hand in a gesture of dismissal. "I'd like to forget it, okay? It really wasn't all that big a deal."

"Hel-lo!" Susan exclaimed, brows arching. "You were assaulted and almost raped, and you don't think it's a big deal? It is to me."

"Forget about it. I have."

"Harry is concerned about you," Susan stressed. "So am I."

Kim tossed up her hands in a gesture of anger. One hand caught the side of her cup, tipping it over and spilling coffee onto the table. "I wish Harry would stop fussing over me like an old mother hen! I'm perfectly capable of taking care of myself." With a quick, impatient movement, she set the cup upright.

Susan stared at her sister, startled by the depths of Kim's anger, and taken aback by her biting remark. "He cares about you. You're like a daughter to him. You lived with him and Maggie for eighteen years."

"He didn't have much choice. I was Maggie's niece so he was stuck with me. She was a good woman, but she was strict and old fashioned. Don't get me wrong, I loved her. After all, she took me in when no one else wanted me."

"That's not true," Susan defended. "Dad wanted to keep you, but he couldn't care for a new born baby himself or find anyone that would."

"Whatever," Kim said with a wave of her hand. Shoving back her chair, she stood up. "I'm going to get dressed. Afterwards, we can catch up on things. I want to hear all about what you've been up to."

"I can tell you about that in two words," Susan said with a dry laugh. "Not much." Since her divorce, she had been like a boxcar sitting on a sidetrack, waiting to get back on the rail and on with her life, but uncertain which switch to flip.

While Kim showered and dressed, Susan wiped up the spilt coffee and wandered back into the living room. Feeling claustrophobic, she pulled open the drapes. Along one wall, a large glass door opened onto the patio, making a dramatic frame for the blue water beyond. Outside, a white wrought-iron table and four chairs were littered with dead leaves, and held the pattern of raindrops long past imprinted in the dust. Alongside them stood several large potted plants sorely in need of water.

Trees that shielded it from the morning sun shaded the living room, with its heavy beige drapery and beige carpet. A thin coat of dust coated the rich-toned, contemporary furniture Kim had selected. Bold patterned pillows lay flat and lifeless on the textured beige sofa. Lined up on the hearth above the stone fireplace were Bill's trophies, the rewards and accolades of his racing skills. The wedding portrait, which had occupied a space alongside them the last time Susan had been here, was conspicuously missing.

At the sound of muffled footfall on the carpeting, Susan turned to see Kim re-entering the room. Her jeans hung loosely from the waistline, and the striped tank top she was wearing bared her long neck and sharp collarbones. Damp from its washing and bearing tooth marks from a comb, her long, straight hair, which she had been bleaching a platinum blond since high school, hung down on her bare shoulders. She gestured for Susan to be seated on the sofa, then slumped onto a large, cushioned chair and swung one leg over the arm.

"So how are you doing since you and Mark called it quits?"

Susan fingered the corner of a throw pillow. "There's no one else, if that's what you're asking. Mark wants us to give our marriage another try."

Kim's dark eyes were cautious. "Is that what you want, too?"

"I'm not sure." During their five-year marriage, Susan had found it easier to acquiesce than to argue with him. It was really one life with two bodies. His life, their bodies. He loved to be in control. Completely. All of the time. But she had become weary of having her life run for her, of not being allowed to make her own decisions.

"You have a choice. I didn't." Kim's voice was weighed with bitterness, She pulled herself erect in the chair.

"It was different with you and Brad," Susan pointed out gently. "His accident...."

"There was nothing accidental about Brad's death!" Kim's brown eyes were like smoldering coals ready to erupt into flames. "Gil Markum killed him."

Susan drew back, horrified at the intensity of her sister's fury. Kim had always been hot tempered, but her anger usually disappeared as fast as it erupted. She had never been consumed with the fiery rage that gripped her now. "Who's Gil Markum?"

"His firm manufactures automotive parts. He wanted to get the jump on his competition by testing a new, souped up carburetor they had developed but wasn't perfected yet. Since Brad was a licensed test-driver, Gil hired him to drive the car. There was a gas leak. The car caught fire and exploded. Brad paid for Gil's greed with his life."

Kim paused, her hands curling into tight fists. "I can't wait until that bastard gets his. I intend to see that he does."

Her sister's pain surged over Susan, leaving a hollowness in her stomach. "I know it's difficult, but you have to forget what happened and move on with your life. I'm sure Brad would want you to."

"I'll never forget what happened to him. Never."

Susan wanted to place her arms around her sister and remind her she wasn't alone, but Kim's stance, the heat of her fury held her back.

"How about the two of us going for a swim?" Susan suggested after a long, weighty moment of silence. "I hope you have an extra suit. Mine is in my suitcase back at Harry's place."

"I think I can find something for you to wear."

Minutes later, the two of them were racing down the stone steps that led onto the beach. The waves, shimmering brightly in the sun, moved toward the shore and lapped gently at the sand. The water was a delight as they plunged into it, sliding with champagne-like tingles through Susan's short hair and along her neck and body. They splashed and dove and swam for short distances, until Susan saw Kim making her way back toward the shore. Following behind, Susan scrambled onto the grass bordering the sand, where the two of them toweled themselves and sat down on the towels.

Leaning back on her arms, her long, wet hair hanging down onto her bare back, Kim lifted her face to the sun.

Susan smiled over at her. "That was great. I haven't gone swimming in a lake since I left here. I hate swimming pools. The chlorine burns my eyes."

Just then a large, yellow dog emerged from the thicket nearby and loped easily along the beach, his huge feet making shallow indentations in the sand. His tongue lolled in the side of his mouth, and his short-furred form gently swayed from side to side.

"By chance, is that the dog that frightened away the guy who attacked you?" Susan asked.

Kim scowled. "That mutt runs around all over the neighborhood. He belongs to the woman who lives behind the trees to your left."

"Lucky for you Rover doesn't stay home." When Kim remained silent, Susan went on. "I saw Reid Elison when I stopped for gas in Lake Center."

Kim's head jerked around. "Him! What did he have to say?"

"He assured me he's still investigating what happened to you."

Kim scowled. "He asks too many questions."

"That's his job. How's he going to find out anything if he doesn't ask questions?"

Rising to her feet, Kim brushed the sand from her pale-skinned body with short, quick whisks of her hand. "Let's go back to the house before I blister."

As they made their way up to the house, Kim pointed across the lake. "See that large house built into the side of the cliff? Gil Markum lives there. Brad built that monstrosity for him. I only need to look across the lake to remember what Gil did to Brad—as if I need a reminder."

Shading her eyes, Susan stopped and peered across the water. She saw a large, sprawling building surrounded by a spacious yard. A dense forest of trees bordered the lawn, grew around it like a protective fence. Like someone signaling with giant mirrors, large glass windows reflected the shine from the sun and sent flashes of light shooting toward them.

"By the way," Susan said as she and Kim continued their progress toward the house. "You almost had another visitor this morning."

Kim head snapped around, and she halted in mid-stride. "What do you mean?"

"As I was turning into your driveway a car behind me signaled to turn, too. The driver must have realized he had the wrong place. He turned off his signal and drove on down the road."

Kim's eyes were wary, her tone apprehensive. "What kind of car was it?"

Susan shrugged. "I didn't pay that much attention. It was an older model. Possibly a Pontiac or an Olds."

"Doesn't sound like anyone I know." Kim took the stone steps that led onto the lawn two at a time. Frowning, Susan followed. Kim's denial had been rushed, hadn't rung true. It had been too hasty. Too definite.

After they changed clothes, the sisters sat down in the living room and chatted causally. As the time passed, Kim began to glance at her watch from time to time, tensed at the slightest sound.

"How long do you intend to be in Lake Center?" she asked.

Susan shrugged. "I'm not sure. Maybe a week."

"Why don't you come out again tomorrow?" Kim suggested after another quick glance at her watch. "Plan to stay overnight. We'll spend a few days together."

Susan sensed that she was being dismissed. "I'd like that. Why don't you come back to Harry's with me and stay the night? I'm sure he'd like to see you. I worry about you alone in this house. After what's happened, aren't you afraid to stay here by yourself? I would be."

"I can take care of myself." Rising, Kim walked across the room where she opened the drawer of a small desk and reached inside. When she withdrew her hand, she was holding a gun. The light from the window struck the hard shiny metal of the handle, and sent a bright shaft of light careening against the wall.

Susan froze at the sight of the cold, steely weapon. She could almost hear the crack of the shot, feel the impact of a bullet piercing her flesh, see bright-red blood spurting. "Do you know how to use that thing?"

"Of course I know how to use it. And I will if I have to."

Susan stared at her sister in disbelief. "Are you saying you think the man who assaulted you will come back?"

"If he does, I'm ready for him."

Chapter 4

▼

"Why don't you get spiffed up and I'll take you out to dinner," Harry said. "All I have in my cupboard is canned soup and pork and beans. I doubt if they're high on your list of favorite foods." The crow's feet at the corners of his faded blue eyes deepened.

Susan laughed lightly. "On the contrary. I live on soup and sandwiches, but I won't turn down a dinner invitation from a good looking man."

In the spare, upstairs bedroom with its old four-poster bed and faded, floral-print wallpaper, she slipped out of the slacks and blouse she had worn out to Kim's place. The spray of warm water was refreshing when she stepped into the shower, but it did not wash away the memory of the gun in Kim's hand or the tone of her voice when she said that she could and would use it if necessary. It had been no ordinary burglary attempt that had taken place at Kim's place, Susan was certain. There was something more to it. Something Kim wasn't telling.

A few minutes later, Susan studied her reflection in the mirror as she touched her mouth with lip-gloss and applied mascara to her lashes. There was a striking resemblance between herself and her sister. They both had large, wide-spaced brown eyes and a wide mouth. But while Kim raced down the streets of life, letting the chips fall where they would, Susan had always inched her way along, as if she were threading her way through a minefield. She was twenty-eight years old but whenever she looked into the mirror, the image of the somber, hungry-for-love girl who had so desperately yearned for someone to care about her leapt out at her. On the surface, however, and in spite of the loneliness and uncertainty since her divorce, she was able to function fairly well.

The day after her high school graduation, her stepmother had told her it was time she fed and clothed herself. Having dreamed for years about the day she could escape, she had shed no tears about leaving. She had gone to St. Paul where she had started working as a receptionist at a prestigious law firm. After attending years of night school to upgrade her skills, she was employed as a paralegal for them now.

"Where are we going for dinner?" she asked her uncle as she entered the living room wearing a slim, blue sheath dress accented with frosty white jewelry.

Harry, too, had showered and changed from faded gabardine slacks and a T-shirt into lightweight trousers, a white shirt, and a sports jacket. "We're dinin' in style. I'm takin' you to The Bayside. Can't say that I'm crazy about the place, but there's not much choice in a town this size."

"I was here for a banquet not long ago," Harry said as they sat across the table from each other. He placed the menu on the edge of the table without looking at it. "The seafood platter was pretty good. I think I'll try it again, but you have whatever you like, Susan."

She closed her menu. "Seafood sounds fine to me."

The lighting was soft and indirect and lush greenery provided a sense of seclusion, she noted as she glanced around the restaurant. The dinner music that filtered through the room was soft and unobtrusive. Candles surrounded by low, amber vases flickered, casting rosy shadows on the tabletop. "This is nice. Why don't you like to come here?"

"Personal reasons," Harry answered gruffly.

After their order had been taken, he turned to Susan. "Now that you've seen Kim, have you figured out what's going on with her?"

Susan took a deep breath. "Not really, except that she's still depressed over Brad's death." She couldn't tell him that Kim had a gun and that she sounded homicidal, at least not yet. Kim had always had a flair for the dramatic. Of exaggeration.

Harry grunted. "For the first time in her life, she's been denied something she wanted, and she can't handle it."

Susan sighed in agreement. "When I was growing up, I envied Kim, almost hated her sometimes. She always seemed to have everything a girl could want." After her mother's death, Susan had remained with her father and been cared for by a succession of housekeepers until he remarried.

While they waited for their dinner to be served, Susan and Harry sipped their Chablis and tried to catch up on the things that had happened in their lives since the last time they had seen each other.

Harry peered across the table from her, his eyes mirroring his curiosity. "So you and your ex are thinkin' about gettin' back together?"

"Mark called several weeks ago. He wants me to come to California, for us to try to work out things. Try again."

"I don't know the guy. Only saw him a couple of times," Harry said. "But he can't be very bright if he let a great gal like you get away."

Susan blinked at the tears that threatened to form in her brown eyes. "I love you, Uncle Harry. You do wonders for a girl's ego."

He placed his gnarled, age-spotted hand atop hers. "You *are* a great gal. You don't always insist on havin' your own way like someone else we both know."

Susan gave him a wry smile. "When I die my epitaph will read '*Here lies Susan. She seldom made waves.*'"

"Oh, I'm sure you have plenty of spunk. But there's nothin' wrong with havin' some respect and consideration for others, too." The glow of the candle on their table colored his wizened face as he pushed back a wisp of gray hair that had fallen onto his forehead. "Unfortunately, if the world were filled with all good guys, it probably wouldn't sell newspapers and I'd be out of a job." He gave Susan a crooked smile.

"As you probably sensed, there was hard feelings between your dad and your Aunt Maggie because she wouldn't give Kim up after he remarried," Harry continued. "Maggie had become attached to her—too attached. She considered Kim *her* daughter. And there was your father's problem with booze, too."

Susan's face darkened in reflection. "When he discovered what a mistake his second marriage was, he tried to drown himself in Jack Daniels. After I left home, I often wondered if he noticed I was gone." She had come back to visit him a number of times, but anesthetized with whiskey, he had barely acknowledged her presence.

"Maggie and I would have taken you in, too, if your dad would have let us have you," Harry reflected quietly.

"I don't know why he didn't," Susan said. "After he started drinking, he scarcely knew I was around. And my stepmother couldn't have cared less. I came with the package when she married my father, so she had to put up with me. But she let me know in no uncertain terms how she felt about me. She was more interested in the money she thought he had. But he took care of that by drinking it all up."

"Maggie did her best to see that you and your sister remained close," Harry said. "But, as you remember, Kim insisted on doing her own thing and to hell with everything and everyone else. I don't mean to bad mouth your sister, but you know how she was. Unfortunately, she hasn't changed much."

Susan released a deep sigh. Kim had often run with the 'in' crowd, and hadn't always acknowledged her older sister's existence unless it enhanced her own image—which it seldom did unless it came to academics.

Harry lifted his glass to his mouth and took a deep swallow of wine. "So are you gonna give your ex another chance?"

Susan tugged at a short strand of brown hair that curved around her ear. "I haven't made up my mind." Since Mark's call suggesting they try for a reconciliation, she had been like a weather vane in a variable wind, swaying first one way and then another. Should she give him another chance or shouldn't she? If she did, would she only be hurt again? Had he changed, as he claimed, or was he still the old, domineering Mark?

"We only go around once so take your time with this," Harry advised in a serious tone.

"Everyone deserves a second chance," Susan defended a trifle sharply. Then regretting her terseness, she apologized. "I'm sorry. I didn't mean to snap at you. I guess this thing with Kim has me on edge."

"You're not the only one." Harry thrust his stubby, gnarled fingers through his thinning hair in a gesture of frustration.

"Maybe I'm apprehensive because I have some doubts if a reconciliation between Mark and me will work," Susan said, thoughtfully sliding her fingers up and down the stem of her wineglass. "That I'm afraid I may only be harboring a foolish illusion." In a way, she was glad she had consented to spend part of her vacation in Lake Center. It gave her time to think, to try to make up her mind about Mark and renewing their relationship.

Not wishing to discuss her personal life any further, she glanced around the restaurant again. "What happened to this place? If I remember correctly, it used to be pretty shabby and the food was terrible."

"The food is great now, in spite of the management," Harry said dryly. "Gil Markum bought this place a couple of years ago. He went all out on the redecoratin', built an addition to the old buildin'."

Susan tensed. Gil Markum—the man Kim held responsible for her husband's death?

"Markum came into Lake Center five or six years ago." Grudgingly, Harry conceded, "He's done a lot for this town. As a matter of fact, he owns a good share of it now. Them that has gets more—any way they can."

Susan frowned. "What does that mean?" When Harry ignored her question, she said, "Kim holds Gil Markum responsible for Brad's death."

Harry's brow knitted. "Why does she think that?"

"I suppose she needs to blame somebody. I didn't know Brad very well, but I remember he was a building contractor who had a penchant for speed and raced cars in his spare time."

Harry nodded. "His company did a lot of construction work for Markum. He built Gil's house and the plant plus several condos for him."

"In spite of what Kim thinks, I'm sure Brad's love for speed and cars is what killed him," Susan rationalized.

At that moment, the waitress arrived with their dinner.

The smell of the food, as it was placed in front of them, filled Susan's nostrils and stirred her taste buds. After the waitress moved away, Susan nibbled on a shrimp. "Ummm! Delicious!"

A half-hour later, when they finished dining and were relaxing over a second glass of wine, Susan saw Harry's attention turn toward the entrance to the restaurant. His eyes were narrowed, and his fingers gripped the stem of his wineglass. "Speakin' of the devil...."

The man who had just entered moved with the suppleness of an athlete, with the gait, certain and fluent, of a man who was in control wherever he found himself. Prematurely white, his hair contrasted sharply with his bronze skin, and thick, dark brows. Over six foot tall, his wide shoulders and muscular forearms strained the seams of his expensive sports coat. Halting, he glanced about the dining room as if he were looking for someone.

"That's Gil Markum?" Susan asked in a hushed tone, unable to look away. Everything about the man stung her imagination with inexplicable fascination.

"In the flesh," Harry growled.

Apparently sensing their gaze, Gil Markum made his way toward the table. His eyes, as he looked at Susan, were sharp and probing. After greeting him coldly, with obvious reluctance, Harry introduced her.

"How do you do, Ms Edwards." Gil's gravelly voice, when he spoke, sounded like two emery boards being rubbed together. Yet Susan found it more sensual than offensive. She judged him to be in his early or mid fifties. The lines of his sun-bronzed face and his hawkish nose served only to augment his handsomeness and give him more character. There was something almost primitive, feral about him as he studied her with his piercing blue eyes.

"Have we met before?" The deceptive softness of his deep voice reminded Susan of the velvet paw-pat of a jungle cat. Yet Susan suspected that underneath his polished demeanor, there were sharp claws that could sprang out for the kill if he were crossed.

A flush spread across Susan's cheeks and into her hairline. "I don't believe so. I'm here on vacation."

He smiled down at her. "Enjoy your evening at The Bayside."

"The food is delicious," she murmured. Feeling like an awkward teenager, she lowered her gaze. Forcing herself to look up again, she met the intensity in his eyes, felt herself wilting under it once again.

Then her gaze was drawn to the lobby where a stunning young woman stood, her gaze searching the room. The short, white dress she was wearing molded the lines of her slender figure, and her raven hair was pulled back and shaped into a chic French knot. Her flawless complexion was a soft bronze shade, undoubtedly the result of carefully measured time in a tanning salon or from lying on some south sea island beach.

Susan stiffened as the woman's cold eyes appraised her in turn from across the room. The look seemed to separate her from the diners seated at the tables surrounding her. Was it her imagination, Susan wondered, or did the woman appear startled for a fleeting moment?

Then she came toward the table, her slim body swaying slightly, like a model on a fashion runway.

Gil, too, watched as the dark-haired woman approached. "I see my lady has arrived," he said. When he turned back to Susan, she found herself once again mesmerized by the intensity of his penetrating gaze. "It was nice meeting you, Ms. Edwards," he said.

Susan's lips parted, but her tongue was paralyzed and her throat constricted, denying her a response.

With a nod to Harry, Gil turned to the brunette woman. Susan watched as the woman tucked her hand into the crook of Gil's arm, and he led her to an isolated table in a far corner of the restaurant.

"Mrs. Markum?" Susan ventured with forced lightness.

"The lady's name is Marisa. She's Mrs. Kyle Markum. Gil has a son. Kyle is the brains of Markum Manufacturin'. Without him, the firm wouldn't be in business. Kyle might be all right if he were given half a chance, but his old man casts a mighty big shadow."

"Is Gil Markum...does he have a wife, too?"

"He's divorced." Harry's voice was succinct. "Careful, darlin'. I don't like that look in your eyes."

Susan flushed. "What look?"

"The look that makes you appear as if you've been struck by lightnin'."

Susan felt as if she had.

Harry's gaze rested on her face for a long moment. "Gil's major league. Little guys like us don't qualify to play in his ball park—not that we play his kind of game."

Chapter 5

▼

The shrill ringing of the telephone made Susan's heart catch with its unexpectedness.

After having breakfast with Harry, she had driven out to Kim's place. They had spent the day together, and had just finished a light evening meal of fruit and salad.

Kim, too, stiffened at the sound of the ring but made no move to answer it. It was almost as if she knew who it was and didn't wish to speak to them.

"Shall I get that?" Susan offered, puzzled by her sister's reaction. "If you like, I can tell whoever it is that you're not home."

"No." Kim's response was immediate. Rising to her feet, she went over to the phone. Placing the receiver to her ear, she listened for several minutes. "I'm sorry," she said to the caller on the other end of the line. "I have company. My sister's here."

Gesturing wildly, Susan tried to attract Kim's attention.

A frown creasing her brow, Kim lowered the phone and covered the mouthpiece with her hand.

"Go on," Susan urged. "Enjoy yourself. I can entertain myself for a little while if you're being invited out. It'll do you good to get out among people."

"I can't leave you here alone," Kim said hesitantly.

"Why not? I don't mind."

Kim held back for a moment, then acquiesced with a light shrug. Speaking into the receiver again, she told whomever was on the line that she would see them in a little while.

Sensing Kim's eagerness, Susan wondered who her sister was talking to. For a moment, Susan questioned the wisdom of what she had done. The fact that her sister thought she needed a gun and had no qualms about using it was disturbing. And yet, Susan reasoned, for a woman living alone and after what had happened, it was an understakable thing to do. What had happened to Kim was a bungled burglary attempt, nothing more, Susan told herself. She was creating mysteries where there were no mysteries. It was incomprehensible that such a thing would happen again and within such a short time. But what if the burglar was determined to do what he had failed to accomplish the first time, and returned to try again?

Chiding herself for allowing her imagination to run away with her, Susan forced the thought aside.

Kim eased her red Firebird down the driveway and onto Ridge Wood Road, the deep, resonant voice of the person who had called her still echoing in her ears. Once her bright, sporty automobile had been a reflection of her feelings, of her life. Vibrant! Exciting! But that was a lifetime ago.

How she had loved Brad; how she hated the man who had taken her husband away from her. Her heart turned to stone whenever she thought about Gil Markum. He had no right to be walking around. Breathing. Laughing. Living his life to the hilt.

She was going to see that he got what he deserved. *Plan revenge; execute same.*

She truly appreciated Susan's concern, but her sister was a little too curious, trying to be a little too 'helpful'. Harry had asked Susan to come here, Kim suspected, to see what was going on with her. He was afraid she was freaking out.

Turning off Ridge Wood Road, Kim drove slowly up a bumpy dirt trail that wound around the south side of Long Lake. Her caller had suggested they rendezvous several miles ahead in a secluded driveway that led up to a vacant farmstead. Filled with chuck holes and covered with overgrown grass and ragweed, the tree-lined road was difficult to access, but discretion was imperative. No one must see them together.

In the beginning, Kim had thought of the man who had called her as a pawn, someone to be used to achieve her goal, a means to an end. But she had altered her course from the original one. Still, that plan might be irreversible. There might not be a way out. But if something did go wrong, she told herself, it was worth it. She would be taking her husband's killer with her.

She wished the man she was meeting hadn't told her he loved her. She didn't want to hurt him. Most of the time, whenever she felt guilt stirring inside her, she quickly thrust it away and replaced it with a picture of black, billowing smoke, a burning car. The sight of a charred body burnt beyond recognition.

Gil Markum was going to pay for what he had done. *Vengeance is mine saith the Lord,* Maggie had often quoted from the Bible. 'Forget it, Lord,' Kim vowed silently. 'I'll take care of this myself.'

Spotting the driveway that led up to the abandoned farmstead, Kim turned onto it, drove up part way and stopped. Minutes later, a dark car pulled alongside her. For fear of being recognized, he drove an older, little used vehicle whenever he came to see her.

In the lengthening shadows of the late evening, she identified his lanky frame and easy manner of walking as he strode through the long grass.

A smile curved his lips as he climbed into her car. Pulling her to him, he kissed her hungrily. "God, how I've missed being with you!" he murmured huskily.

For a brief moment, Kim wondered if she should have left Susan alone at the house, if she were safe. Then all was forgotten.

Chapter 6

After Kim left, Susan dialed Harry's number and they chatted for a short time. When she hung up, feeling restless and uneasy in the unfamiliar surroundings, she glanced at her watch as she switched on the table lamps. It was almost nine o'clock, but there was still plenty of light. It lingered at this time of the year, as if it were reluctant to let go of the day.

Taking a small scarf she found hanging in the coat closet near the doorway, she pulled the ends under her hair and tied it. Draping a light sweater over her shoulders to protect herself in case the mosquitos were out, she went through the patio door. Since the door was in back of the house and she did not plan to be gone long or go far, she did not lock it.

As she wandered along the beach, the breeze gently lifted the fringe of bangs on her forehead. Savoring the tranquility, she walked on for a quarter of a mile, oblivious to any sound except the washing of the waves and the soft shifting of her shoes in the sand. The setting sun painted the lake in a soft coral, and here and there a fishing boat drifted on the water. The area around Long Lake, unlike Lake Sally, which bordered the village of Lake Center, was not extensively developed or populated. As she strolled along the water's edge, Susan's gaze lifted to the spot where Gil Markum lived. The moment she had seen him the previous night, she had been caught up in the aura of the man, like a sliver of steel to a powerful magnet.

Her thoughts interrupted by the sharp barking of a dog, she halted and looked about. The sound came from the dense growth of trees that adjoined Kim's property.

In the waning twilight, Susan saw an elderly woman standing motionless near the edge of the woods. A big yellow dog stood alongside her, barking furiously in Susan's direction. It looked like the dog that had been on the beach the day before when she and Kim were swimming.

The woman lifted her hand and waved. Returning the gesture, Susan walked over to her.

The elderly woman patted the dog on the head, and urged him to be quiet. The print, short-sleeved blouse she was wearing hung on the outside of her loose-fitting slacks, and her white hair was permed into a mass of tight curls. "I thought you were Kim," she said to Susan.

"I'm her sister." Susan explained that Kim had gone out for the evening.

After introducing herself as Esther Helgeson, the elderly woman invited Susan to come up to her place and have a cup of coffee with her. "I'm all alone," she said. "I enjoy having someone to talk to."

Susan hesitated, but under the older woman's persistent urging, she relented. "I can't stay long. I left the back door unlocked."

As Susan followed her up the narrow, wooded path that led to her house, Esther told her she hadn't seen Kim lately.

"I don't think she goes out much," Susan said. "She's still depressed over the death of her husband."

"That's understandable," Esther empathized. "I was lost when Henry passed on three years ago. Still am. And there's that other thing that happened to Kim, too. Makes me edgy living here by myself. I'm glad I got Butch."

Entering the kitchen via the back door, Esther motioned for Susan to be seated on a painted wooden chair alongside a small, drop-leafed table. The small room was as weathered and inviting as its owner. The window beside the table was framed with sunny yellow pricilla curtains, and several pots of red begonias sat on the sill.

"I don't like the idea of Kim being alone all the time," Susan said as the older woman filled two cups with thick, black coffee.

"I never know what's going on at her place." Esther sat down across from Susan, her thin, bony fingers curled around her cup. "It's hard to see through the woods with all the leaves on the trees. But sometimes Butch barks in that direction." Bending down, Esther patted the head of the huge dog that sat on his haunches beside the table, eyeing Susan with friendly curiosity. At the touch of his mistress's hand, his bushy tail swished back and forth on the worn vinyl floor.

"It's lucky for Kim you have Butch." Susan said. "I understand he scared her assailant away."

Esther beamed proudly. "Butch's size scares people, but his bark is worse than his bite."

The fact that Kim didn't want to talk about the incident baffled Susan. Quite possibly, she conceded, Kim's avoidance of the subject made the occurrence more provoking than it really was.

Susan took a swallow of coffee. "Are you certain you didn't see or hear anything that day?"

Esther's lined brow pulled into a reflective frown. "Not that I can recall, but my memory ain't what it used to be."

"I wish someone had seen or heard something," Susan emphasized. "The authorities don't seem to know what happened or be able to find the person responsible. What happened to Kim may not be a big deal to them or my sister, but it is to me. I don't like the idea of her getting beaten up on her own doorstep."

"Wait a minute...." Esther interrupted, her faded eyes suddenly alert. "My grandson was visiting me that day. Maybe he heard something that could help."

Susan's heart missed a beat. "Could I talk to him?"

"He's away at camp right now."

Susan's hopes tumbled. "Maybe you could ask him about it the next time you see him?"

"I'll do that," Esther promised. "He'll be home in a day or two. I'm sure he'll be out to visit me."

"The thought that the person who assaulted my sister is still out there walking around, possibly to do it again bothers me," Susan said. "If I'm not here and if your grandson does remember something…<u>anything</u>, would you call the sheriff's office? It might help them in their investigation."

Esther nodded. "I'm just as anxious to catch that guy as you are."

A glance out the window revealed that the sun had slid behind the horizon and the evening was quickly darkening into night. Although she was less than a half mile from Kim's place, she didn't relish the idea of walking back in the dark. The person who had assaulted and tried to rape her hadn't been apprehended yet. He could be out there somewhere, waiting to strike again. Lying in wait for his next victim.

Stop that! Susan reprimanded herself. *No one's going to bother you. You'll be perfectly safe.*

She stood up from her chair. "I'd better be getting back. I didn't realize it was this late."

The moon, partially covered by a drifting cloud now and then, bathed the lake in liquid gold as she made her way back down the beach. She paused to take a deep breath and savor the clean night air. Since the sand persisted in spilling into her shoes, she removed them. Tying the laces together, she carried the shoes in her hand as she proceeded down the beach. Feeling a sense of being immersed in the night, with its soft night noises and the water lapping gently at the shore, her uneasiness began to slip away. What a beautiful setting. What a beautiful night. What possible danger could be lurking in its shadows?

Then, the hair prickling on the nape of her neck, she spun around at the sound of footfalls shuffling in the sand behind her. Outlined in the moonlight, she saw a grotesque creature moving toward her. It was huge and towering and clothed in black. In the depths of the night, its face was a cadaverous blur beneath a dark, narrow brimmed cap.

Chapter 7

Chief Deputy Reid Elison sat at his desk wondering what the night held in store. Although Lake Center was a small town, it had its share of robberies, muggings, and domestic violence. Since he had come back, he had participated in a major drug bust. Signs of the times, he thought, releasing a weighty sigh. He hated to see it.

After meeting Susan Edwards at the gas station, the Hastings case had been thrust back into the forefront. Although he'd put the report in the files and gone on to other things, the case had remained on the edge of his mind. Hastings had reported the assault, but when he went to investigate, she provided him with little information. It was as if she didn't particularly care if the perpetrator was apprehended or not. Her sister seemed more concerned about what had happened than the victim had.

The ringing of the telephone on his desk sliced into Reid's thoughts.

"Just received a call from a woman who said she was chased along the beach, that someone tried to drown her," the dispatcher told him. "She's afraid the guy might still be there."

"What's the location?" Reid asked, suddenly alert.

"22582 Ridge Wood Road—the Kim Hastings place."

Reid's gripped tightened on the phone. "Are you sure?"

"That's the address she gave me."

"What the hell's going on out there anyway?" Shoving back his chair, Reid made for the door.

Chapter 8

Susan released a ragged sigh of gratitude as the patrol car swung into the yard, red lights flashing in the darkness. Her fingers were numb and her arms ached from holding the gun and pointing it toward the patio door for so long. As she waited for what had seemed eons, she'd told herself over and over that this wasn't happening. That it was all a crazy nightmare and she would wake up any minute.

Opening the door in response to a knock, she stepped back. The uniformed officer stood in the doorway. Removing his hat, he held it in his hand. His mouth, beneath his dark mustache, was unsmiling. It was then that she recognized Reid Elison.

"Oh, it's you."

"Sorry to disappoint you, but I'm on night duty this week," he said as he stepped inside. "Are you the one who called in?"

"I'm here visiting my sister," Susan explained. "Someone tried to strangle me, to drown me as I walked on the beach a little while ago,"

Reid's keen gaze swept around the room, taking in everything—the chair where she had been sitting, the sofa, the furnishings, the shadows that lurked in the corners. His inspection ended with another sharp appraisal of Susan. "Where's your sister?"

Angered by his abrupt manner, Susan struggled for a semblance of politeness. "She's out for the evening."

"You're here by yourself?"

"Yes. I urged her to go. I didn't know that my life would be in danger."

Reid's cold eyes flickered over Susan's five-foot-six frame. "After what happened to your sister, do you think it was wise to stay here alone?"

"Kim stays here by herself...she thinks the break-in attempt was a one time thing...." Puzzled by her sister's odd behavior when she had received the phone call, Susan admitted to herself that she hadn't been thinking when she had urged Kim to go out. She had been more concerned about her sister's social life than her own safety.

Reid's penetrating gray eyes narrowed beneath his thick brows. "Tell me what happened to you."

Susan's chin tilted up several inches. Haltingly, she told him about the attack on the beach. Before she was finished, she saw a flicker of doubt flit across Reid's face.

"Did you see the guy's face?" he wanted to know.

"It was too dark." Shivering, Susan wrapped her arms around herself, barely conscious that she was still holding the gun in her hand. "I don't have the faintest idea why anyone would do something like that. He could have killed me if he had wanted to. I couldn't have stopped him. He was big. Very strong. Things like this don't happen in Lake Center."

Reid's face was a rugged terrain of planes and shadows as he studied her in the lamp light. A frown deepened the creases on his forehead.

Bewildered by the doubt mirrored in the frosty depths of his shrewd gray eyes, Susan asked, "What's wrong?"

"You say this guy was large and wore dark clothing?"

"That's right."

"But you didn't see his face?"

"It was too dark," Susan said once again, a trifle sharply this time. What was Reid getting at? Then she remembered he'd told the gas station attendant that Kim had been uncooperative when he had investigated the assault on her. That she had been vague about the man's description.

"Did the guy say anything to you?" Reid asked.

Susan repeated the words her assailant had uttered. *Mess with me, Bitch, and you'll pay.* He must have mistaken her for Kim, Susan determined. What had Kim done to ignite such fury? Why would someone want to harm her?

Reid's countenance tightened. He spoke carefully, searchingly. "And the guy chased you and choked you? Then all of a sudden, released you and vanished into the darkness?"

"That's right." Susan's nerves were already raw, threadbare. She didn't need this—to be treated as if she were the criminal instead of the victim.

"Are you doubting what happened to me just as you obviously doubt my sister's report about the assault on her?" Susan's dark eyes were obsidian, smoldering in rising irritation. "Is that why this…this creep, whoever he is, is still free, still going around attacking people?"

There was an edge to Reid's voice as he spoke. "Sometimes a woman has a fight with her boyfriend or her husband, and things get a little violent. She calls the cops, but afterwards, she has second thoughts or she's too embarrassed to tell the truth. Maybe he's threatened to do it again if she tells what happened so she comes up with this cock-and-bull story about being beaten up by a stranger."

"I don't have a boyfriend or a husband," Susan said tersely. "And I don't like being called a liar."

"I didn't say you were."

"You implied it. You think that Kim and I are a couple of nuts making up stories to keep the sheriff's department busy. That we're wasting your time."

"I didn't say that."

"I doubt if Kim tried to break into her own house or rape herself." Susan paused, choking on her rage. "I certainly didn't try to strangle myself."

The muscles bunched along Reid Elison's square jaw, giving him a forbidding look. "I told you your sister's case is still under investigation."

"And in the meantime, practically the same thing has happened again. I know it was only an *attempted* burglary, an *attempted* rape. Those things may not be high on your priority list, but they are on mine. That man who chased me on the beach wanted me dead. I could feel it in his grip. I could hear it in his voice." She was angrier than she had been in her entire life. She hadn't thought she was capable of such anger, had never been so accusative or combative toward anyone.

"You've got it all wrong." Reid's tone was adamant as his voice sliced through her damning speech. "Your sister's case hasn't been swept under the rug as you so ardently believe."

"So you said before."

"Do you have somewhere else to go for the rest of the night?" The words were spoken so precisely, so quietly that Susan knew he was fighting to keep a rein on his temper.

Sparks literally ignited in the semi-darkness of the room as her fiery brown eyes met his stormy gray ones. "I'll be okay. Kim will be home any time. After what's just happened, I don't want her spending the night alone."

"I'll check the grounds," Reid said after a moment. "But I suspect that whoever was out there is long gone by now."

Reid was absent about ten minutes. "There doesn't seem to be anyone around," he said when he re-entered the house. "I'll be back in the morning to check out the beach and see if I can find anything. Lock up good. Be sure you know what you're shooting at before you use that thing."

"What...?" Susan stammered in bewilderment.

He pointed to the gun she was still holding in her hand, as if it were a permanent part of her.

She glared at him, warm spots of color staining her cheeks.

After he was gone, she locked the door, checking it twice to make certain it was secure. Minutes later, still dressed, she lay down on the bed in the guestroom. Her hand rested on the handle of the gun that she had placed under the pillow. Her ears were peeled for sounds in the darkness; stealthy footsteps, the furtive creaking of a door opening, the shattering of the glass patio door. Once she thought she heard footsteps outside the window near her bed, and her breathing stopped. Her grasp tightened on the cold, steely handle of the gun.

A half-hour later, she heard Kim come home and go into her bedroom.

Still sleep eluded Susan. Nightmarish images crowded into her mind, vivid splashes of unsummoned dreams. She saw a huge figure moving inexorably toward her. Chasing her. Choking her.

"You'll pay, Bitch. You'll pay!" His words cut through her like a knife, draining the blood from her body.

When she finally fell asleep, the figure continued to pursue her in her dreams. She was running, the sound of her footfall echoing hollowly. She was getting tired, slowing to a crawl. He was closing in on her. No! No! There was something relentless about the way he was chasing her, like a wolf after a wounded deer.

She tried to scream, but there was no breath left in her body. Helplessly, numbly, she looked about for an avenue of escape. She saw none.

Then, swooping down on her like a hawk, her pursuer lifted her into his arms. She couldn't see his face. "No! No!"

When she tried to beat at him, to escape his grasp, she was trapped by the strength of his burly arms, in the bedcovers that bound her like ropes.

Drenched with perspiration, she bolted upright. Had she screamed aloud? Her heart was pounding like a jackhammer. She struggled to free herself from the sheet that was tangled around her legs, holding her captive like the hands of the man who had tried to strangle her.

Chapter 9

▼

"Morning," Kim greeted as she came into the kitchen. Her backless bedroom slippers flip-flopped on her feet, and her short, cotton robe was belted loosely around her waist. She stretched, then yawned lazily. Her countenance was still rumpled with sleep, and her long, platinum hair softly tousled.

"I made a pot of coffee," Susan said. "Would you like some?" She had tied a sheer scarf around her neck to cover the faint, purplish mark on her throat.

Aware that Reid Elison would be arriving any minute, she knew she must tell her sister what had happened the night before. Placing a cup of coffee in front of Kim who sat down across the table from her, Susan gave her sister a brief account of the harrowing experience.

"Oh, no!" Spilling coffee over the side, the cup dropped from Kim's grasp and onto the table top with a sharp clatter. There was open fright in her eyes.

"I think he mistook me for you. It could have been the man who assaulted you."

"No. It couldn't have been." Kim's response was quick. Adamant.

"How can you be so sure?" Susan wanted to know.

Kim's guard was up again, her face unfathomable. "It was probably some weirdo wandering along the beach."

"I don't think so." Susan doubted that she had been a random target, confronted by a stranger going for a casual, nighttime stroll along the beach, whose raging hormones had gotten the better of him. His words were too personal, as if he knew exactly who he was talking to—or thought he did. The idea that someone wanted to hurt her or her sister sent chills washing over her, from the soles of her feet to her fingertips. "He threatened me, tried to kill me."

"What!" Color had risen to tinge Kim's cheeks. There was fear in her voice.

"Kim," Susan asked apprehensively, "Are you in some sort of trouble?"

"Don't be ridiculous! Like I said, it must have been some weirdo walking along the beach. I'm not leaving you in this house alone again, day or night. I should have known...."

"What about you?" Susan pointed out. "You shouldn't stay here by yourself either. It's too risky."

"I'll be all right. I have a gun, remember?"

As Susan studied her sister's face, she sensed that Kim wasn't as confident as she was pretending to be. She dabbed at the spilled coffee with a paper napkin, tossed it aside and seized another from the napkin holder. Swiped it around the tabletop.

A knock sounded on the door, ending their conversation and Kim's nervous reaction. When she opened the door, Reid Elison's huge frame filled the doorway. Susan felt the forceful nature that he emanated, the careful control he exhibited over his emotions.

He entered the room, his gaze taking in the scarf around her neck. "Have you thought of anyone who would want to harm you?"

"I haven't lived around here in years. I don't think many people know I'm in town. And even if they do, I can't think of a reason for anyone to threaten me or want to harm me."

"Go over what happened to you again." His keen gaze fastened on her face, Reid listened closely as she gave him an abbreviated account of what had taken place on the beach the previous night.

"Have you noticed any strangers loitering about lately…anything out of the ordinary since the assault on you?" he asked Kim.

"This is supposed to be private property," she pointed out.

"That doesn't mean much to some people." Reid turned back to Susan. "I'd like to go down to the beach. You can show me where the attack took place."

As they proceeded across the lawn and down the stone steps to the lake, Susan noted he had shortened his stride to accommodate her. He was hatless, and the breeze stirred his thick, curly hair.

"I thought you were on night duty," she said.

"This is my case. I'm the one who came out here when your sister was accosted earlier, the one who responded to your call last night."

"So you haven't had any sleep yet."

"I'm used to it," he answered as they stepped onto the sandy beach.

The memory of her terrifying experience, which had been with Susan throughout the night, robbing her of sleep, had still been with her when she awakened. It was jolted anew now, as she spotted her light, summer sweater and tennis shoes, splattered with sand and lying near the edge of the lake.

All around, the beach had been churned and ridged, but there wasn't one distinguishable footprint. Susan watched Reid as he walked slowly up and down the beach, head bent, eyes intent and probing. If he noticed anything relevant, he gave no indication.

"Do you think what happened to me last night is related to what happened to Kim?" Susan asked as they made their way back to the house.

Reid's thick brows knitted. "There's so little to go on. Like you, your sister couldn't give me much of a description of the man who accosted her. It could be the same man. It could be someone else."

This wasn't Phoenix or St. Paul where small matters like burglaries and break-ins were seldom pursued because they took officers away from more vital concerns. This was Lake Center where such things were considered crimes. Susan conceded that the break-in attempt might not be looked at as a serious crime, but the attempted rape certainly should be. Yet, strangely, Kim didn't seem interested in pursuing it.

"I want to know who attacked me last night and why," Susan persisted. "And in spite of what you and Kim seem to think, I believe she's still in danger. There's something funny going on here."

"I agree," a grave-faced Reid echoed.

Susan combed her fingers through her short brown hair. "Kim isn't herself. I'm as concerned about her emotional state as I am about her physical safety."

"Has she talked to you about the assault?"

Susan shook her head. "I'm the one who has to bring it up. She sloughs it off, doesn't want to discuss it."

For a moment, Susan considered confiding in him her fears about Kim and Kim's mental state. How she had vowed to use her gun if she had to. How she had sworn vengeance against Gil Markum, but Susan held back. She had always reserved a part of herself, like a reservoir to go to for strength—or a place to hide in. She had never had anyone to go to, to confide in, and to share her dreams or her fears with. Not even Mark. He would have considered her sillier and more inept than he already did. If she expressed her concerns to Reid, he would probably feel the same way. And unsure of his ability or commitment, she did not fully trust him.

Susan recalled the expression on her sister's face when Kim had spoken of Gil Markum. The coldness. The burning hatred. Unconsciously, she shivered. She felt the warmth of Reid's hand on her bare arm.

"Are you okay?" His eyes searched her face.

"I can't forget the look on Kim's face sometimes. I have the strangest feeling there's more to all of this than meets the eye."

"So do I." The sternness that had been on Reid's face when he arrived had softened. "Maybe we'll get lucky and come up with something soon."

In the face of his more considerate manner toward her, Susan apologized for her behavior the previous night.

Reid gave her a crooked smile. "I empathize with your frustration. And I guess I was a little abrupt, too. I've been doing double duty lately, and I'm not in the best of moods at times."

When they reached the squad car that he had parked on the edge of the front lawn, Reid stood with his hand on the door handle. "I want you and your sister to take extra precautions until we get to the bottom of this. Perhaps the two of you could stay somewhere else for a few days."

"Our uncle, Harry Risland, has been trying to talk her into moving into town. So far, she's refused to leave this place."

"Harry's your uncle?" Reid said, his brows arching.

"Do you know him?"

"Everyone knows everyone else in a town this size, remember?" Taking a deep breath, Reid urged, "Work on Kim. Maybe you can talk her into staying at Harry's place for a while."

After Reid drove away, the picture of him walking back and forth through the sand, eyes alert and probing, hips trim and lean in his uniform, returned to Susan's mind. He had *seemed* genuinely concerned, thorough in his investigation.

When she entered the house, she saw that Kim had changed from her robe into jeans and a knit top that clearly defined her small, braless breasts. She was standing in front of the living room window, staring out. It struck Susan that her sister spent a great deal of time, too much, staring broodingly into space, her mind obviously in a deep, dark world of vengeful thoughts.

Kim turned around. "Find anything?"

When Susan shook her head, her sister released a weighty breath. Seemed relieved.

"I don't think what happened to me last night was a random incident," Susan persisted. Although she knew Kim didn't want to pursue the subject, it was too important to dismiss. "I think whoever was out there thought he was chasing you. Is there something you haven't told me about the break-in? Are you sure you aren't in some kind of trouble?"

"What makes you think that?" Kim said in quick dismissal. "The creep who tried to break in was some bum who, undoubtedly, knew I lived alone and thought I was an easy mark. That I had a few bucks lying around."

Susan's teeth bit down on her lip, a habit she had acquired when she was a child and under stress. Once again Kim was dismissing what had happened in an off-handed manner. She was being a little too apathetic, treating the situation with too much indifference. As she'd done previously, Susan sensed that Kim's depression, her peculiar behavior, and the attempted break-in and rape, were somehow a part of the same scenario.

"So you can't think of any reason why someone would want to harm you?" Susan pressed. "Perhaps someone from a long time ago, when Brad was alive or before you met him?"

Kim's eyes narrowed in annoyance. "It was just some petty thief."

Why didn't her sister want to discuss the assault? Susan wondered. Why was she being so cavalier about it?

"I'm sorry about what happened to you last night," Kim said. "You'd better go back into town and stay with Harry."

"And leave you alone? No way."

"I'll be okay. I have a gun."

"The gun isn't going to do you any good if someone breaks in and attacks you while you're asleep."

"That's not going to happen."

"I didn't think someone was going to attack me on the beach either."

"All right. All right," Kim relented. "But I'm going to drive my own car into town. I want to be free to come and go as I please. This is my home. No pervert is going to drive me out of it."

Chapter 10

Susan held out a knit, striped green top for Kim to see. "How do you like this?"

Insisting that she drive her car to the supermarket for groceries so they could prepare dinner at Harry's place, Kim had stopped by the town's new shopping mall and offered to show Susan around.

Kim spoke from behind the rack of clothing she was browsing through in the small boutique. "Why don't you try it on?"

As she pushed aside the curtain and stepped into the dressing room, Susan collided with a slender young woman who was coming out of one of the stalls with several articles of clothing draped over her arm.

"I'm sorry!" Susan exclaimed. It was then that she saw the glistening green eyes and recognized Marisa Markum. Susan's first impression of Gil Markum's daughter-in-law had been that she was a cold and sophisticated woman. Now, in designer jeans and a brief, bare midriff top that clung to her youthful figure, and her ebony hair falling casually around her beautiful face, she looked as if she were scarcely out of her teens. But in spite of her casual appearance, the cold chill was still in her chryolite eyes.

"I see that you know Kim Hastings," Marisa said.

"She's my sister," Susan explained. "Do you know her?"

"I know *of* her."

"I suppose everyone around Lake Center has heard about the assault she experienced,"

"It certainly made a good story, didn't it?"

Susan's brows knitted. "What do you mean?"

"Just what I said—it made a good story. For what purpose, I haven't quite figured out yet. Have they ever found that so-called burglar? Of course not. They never will because he doesn't exist." With those words, Marisa shoved past Susan and out of the fitting room.

Because of the animus Kim displayed whenever the Markum name was uttered, Susan was reluctant to tell her about the encounter in the dressing room. But the raven-haired woman's remarks weighed on Susan's mind as Kim drove her Firebird away from the mall.

"Do you know Marisa Markum?" Susan asked, glancing over at Kim.

Kim's head jerked around. "How do you know Marisa? Why are you asking about her?"

"No particular reason," Susan hedged. "She was in the boutique where we were."

"I didn't see her. Marisa is Gil's darling—a senator's daughter, no less. It's always convenient to have one in the family. It opens lots of doors, helps cover up a lot of dirty deals."

Kim's countenance was grim, her mouth pinched and narrow. "But Gil isn't going to get away with what he did to Brad."

"If you feel so strongly that he's responsible for Brad's death, why don't you file a lawsuit against him?" Susan reasoned. "Our office handles those kinds of cases all the time."

"I don't want his money. I want his blood."

The venom in the remark sent a shiver up Susan's spine. "What good will that do? No one gains anything by being vengeful. All it does is revive their own pain. They often end up hurting themselves more than they hurt the other person. Put the past behind you and move on with your life."

"Not until the old one is ended." There was a resoluteness, a finality in Kim's voice. "Don't you know revenge is the sweetest passion, sister, dear?"

After dinner that night, afraid he would hear about it from someone else, Susan told Harry what had happened to her on the beach the previous evening. She downplayed the incident, euphemizing it as not to worry Harry as much.

"Not you too!" Harry looked over at Kim. "What the hell's goin' on out there?"

She lifted her shoulders in a shrug. "I have no idea."

Susan could see that Harry wanted to pursue the matter, that he didn't believe Kim. Obviously aware that it was useless to question Kim, he said no more, but frustration was apparent on his lined face.

In her mind, Susan could still hear the unrelenting thud of her attacker's feet in the shifting sand, feel the pressure of his powerful fingers tightening around her throat like steel bands.

When Susan awakened the next morning, she was disconcerted for several minutes. Then her confusion peeled off and fell away. There was a dull ache in her body, from her toes to the top of her head. It was the result of emotional rather than physical pain, she knew. Kim's behavior was disturbing. Difficult to understand.

After a long shower, during which she let the warm spray of water stream over her in an effort to wash away the weariness in her body and her mind, Susan dressed and entered the kitchen to discover that Harry had already left for work.

There was a note on the table.

'Remembered the TV repairman is coming today or tomorrow,' the note read. *'If I don't come back, don't worry. I'll be okay.'* Kim

Susan wanted to leap into her Skyhawk and race out to her sister's place to protect her from an undefinable adversary. But she knew she had to restrain the impulse. Put aside her fears. Kim had made it clear she didn't think she was in any danger. If her sister didn't want to be helped, there was little she could do for her, Susan conceded. She couldn't stay indefinitely. If matters didn't change drastically in the next day or so, Kim would have to solve her own problems—whatever they were.

Uncertain how she would spend the day, Susan washed the dishes she used at breakfast plus the ones Harry had left in the sink. There was no automatic dishwasher. Maggie had believed doing things the hard way gave them more importance. As Susan was wiping the kitchen counters, the phone rang.

"How would you and your sister like to join me for lunch at Miller's Cafe?" Harry wanted to know. "My treat."

"Kim's gone back home," Susan told him. "But I'll take you up on your invitation."

After applying a coat of make-up to cover the bruising on her throat, she slipped into a pair of beige slacks and the striped top she had purchased at the mall. As she entered the cafe a short time later, she saw it was filled to capacity. The aroma of freshly baked pies and burgers and onions tingled in her nostrils. Susan remembered the Ma and Pa business from when she was a teenager. Run by the same people, according to the sign in front, and sporting the same homey ambiance, it appeared as if it were still going strong. Then, in the center of the room, she spied her uncle sitting at one of several small tables that were surrounded by booths. Across from him, Susan saw a pair of wide shoulders in a navy uniform, a shock of dark, springy hair.

Spotting her, Harry stood up and motioned.

"The place is filled up so I invited Reid to sit with me," Harry explained when Susan reached the table.

Giving her a nod of acknowledgment, Reid rose to his feet. "It was nice talking to you, Harry. I'll leave you and your niece to enjoy your lunch." There was an aloofness about him once again. It was as if he were placing the image of an officer of the law between himself and others, as though he wanted to keep them at a distance.

"There's no empty booths or tables so you may as well sit down." Harry stood up and motioned for Susan to sit down on the chair next to him, then sat down again. "I've already had lunch. I've got to go back to work in a few minutes. Somethin's come up. You and Reid'll have to keep each other company."

Reluctantly, the deputy eased himself back onto the chair. When the waitress appeared several minutes later, with hesitation, he ordered two cheeseburgers and a cup of black coffee. Susan ordered iced tea and a chef's salad with ranch dressing.

Swallowing the last of his coffee, Harry stood up. "Do you plan to go out to Kim's later?"

Susan shrugged. "I don't know. I'll have to call her and find out if she's coming back into town."

Reaching into his wallet, Harry pulled out a twenty-dollar bill and tossed it on the table. "Lunch for the two of you is on me."

As Harry walked away, Susan turned to Reid. "Looks like you're stuck with my company until there's an empty table."

A tinge of pink colored his cheeks. "I'm sorry if I gave you the impression that I didn't want to sit with you."

Finding his discomfort amusing, a half-smile curved Susan's lips.

He took a drink from his water glass. After a long, obvious moment, he said, "Harry told me you and your sister spent the night at his place."

"Kim resents being fussed over," Susan said. "But I feel uneasy about her staying out at her house alone."

"She's either got a lot of guts or she's a damned fool."

"It's her home," Susan reasoned to herself as much as to the man across from her. "Although it upsets me that she went back there alone, I understand her doing so. I'm not sure if I would be that brave."

After a moment, in an effort to fill the lengthy silence that hovered between them, Susan asked, "How do you like living in Lake Center again?"

Reid shrugged. "It's okay."

"Does your family still live here?"

"My parents do, My two brothers live back east."

"I remember them. They were both older than you." Susan envied anyone who had been raised in a close knit family. Kim, who was the only family she had left, seemed to hold her away, to be so consumed with vengeance that she didn't have time or room in her life for anyone or anything else. "Do you plan to stay in Lake Center?" Susan asked when Reid made no effort to continue the conversation.

"The local sheriff is retiring this fall," he answered. "I'm thinking of running for the office."

The appearance of the waitress bearing their lunch interrupted the conversation between them. As the waitress placed the cheeseburgers in front of him, Reid explained that he hadn't eaten since the previous evening.

"Is this your usual fare?" Susan's comment was made with a half-smile.

"It keeps me going."

"That's what I used to tell Mark whenever he criticized my eating habits." She hadn't intended to bring up her personal life. Evoked by the savory smell of the food he had ordered, the comment had slipped out. She had wolfed down more than one serving of tasty, saturated fat food when she was out of Mark's sight. Admittedly, just for spite most of the time. To prove to herself that she wasn't completely controlled.

Reid's brows arched as he placed his sandwich back on the plate after taking a bite. "Who's Mark?"

"My ex-husband. I've been told I'm lucky he's out of my life."

"But you're not convinced of that, right?"

Spearing a piece of lettuce, Susan lifted the leafy green to her mouth and chewed it thoroughly. Ignoring the comment, she said, "Harry told me Linda passed away. I'm sorry." Susan hoped she wasn't being too intrusive, but she didn't want to discuss Mark or their relationship.

"Linda's been gone almost two years." There was a bitterness, a longing in Reid's tone and on his face. Inexplicably, Susan wanted to reach out to him, to comfort him, but she held back. She sensed that this strong, grief-stricken man did not want her pity.

They sat in silence for several minutes, preoccupied with their individual memories and the food before them.

Susan took a swallow of iced tea, then placed the glass on the table. "Do you know Marisa Markum?"

"We don't exactly move in the same social circles, but I know who she is. Why?"

"Are she and her husband happily married?"

"I wouldn't know. But it shouldn't be too difficult being married to someone who looks like Marisa Markum."

Susan shot him a look of disdain. "A typical male response."

Reid's mouth curved into a half-smile. A twinkle shone in his eyes. Then he sobered. "Why are you asking me if I know Marisa Markum?"

"No reason," Susan replied quickly. "I recently met her, that's all." She didn't intend to tell him that Marisa had insinuated the break-in attempt at Kim's was a fabrication. Haunted by Kim's swift response to label what had happened on the beach as a random incident, and in no way connected to the break-in, Susan wondered if withholding information, no matter how trivial or doubtful she considered it to be, was the prudent thing to do. Underneath Kim's dismissal, Susan had sensed her sister's doubts, her rising fear.

"Are you all right?" Reid's voice interjected into Susan's thoughts. "You look...."

"Worried?" Susan asked. "I am."

"I want you to know that I *will* find out what's been going on at your sister's place if it's the last thing I do." Sincerity was registered on Reid's face. For the first time, Susan felt that he considered it important, that he truly cared about what had happened to her and her sister. She prayed her concern for her sister was unnecessary and unwarranted, as Kim insisted it was. It was obvious it wasn't appreciated.

Suddenly aware of Reid's woodsy aftershave, she saw the resolve in his slate gray eyes. She wanted to say something light to rid herself of the dread that had descended on her, but words eluded her. For an instant, she found herself wanting to be held. To be told that what had happened to her on the beach had been a bad dream and actually hadn't occurred at all. But it had. And although she and Kim hadn't been close as siblings, Susan knew she was a part of this scenario, whether or not her sister wanted her to be.

A short time later, as she and Reid were bidding each other goodbye outside the restaurant, a low-slung, late-model sports car pulled over to the curb alongside them. In it was a sandy haired man in his mid or late thirties. His chin was hidden by a neatly trimmed beard a shade or so darker than his hair.

Pocketing his car keys, the man stepped onto the sidewalk. Of average build, he was wearing lightweight slacks and a matching blazer that hadn't been purchased at the local department store, Susan was certain. He nodded to Reid, asked, "How's it goin'?"

After returning the greeting, Reid said, "Susan, I'd like you to meet Kyle Markum. Kyle, Susan Edwards."

"Hello." Kyle's smile was warm, affable as he shook her hand.

So this was the man whose father, according to Harry, cast too big a shadow for him to have an identity of his own, Susan thought. Kyle was several inches shorter and not as broad or muscular as the barrel-chested Gil. Nor was he as strikingly handsome or charismatic. He was definitely not as intimidating.

"Do you live here in Lake Center, Ms Edwards?" Kyle asked.

"I was born and raised here," Susan answered. "But I live in St. Paul now. Perhaps you know my sister, Kim Hastings. I'm visiting her for a few days."

A flicker of surprise flitted across Kyle's bearded face. Then a more guarded look replaced it. "I've met your sister. I knew her husband slightly."

Susan had the definite feeling that she had just shook hands with the man who had been signaling to turn into Kim's driveway the day she had arrived, but had changed his mind at the last moment. But what would Kyle Markum be doing at Kim's place?

Chapter II

Still thinking of Kyle Markum, Susan made her way toward the spot in the parking lot where she had left her car. A gleaming white Lincoln Continental was parked alongside her Skyhawk, dwarfing it. Slowing her progress, she viewed the Lincoln with admiring eyes. Who in Lake Center could own such an expensive automobile?

"Ms Edwards—Susan, isn't it?" Susan's pulse quickened at the sound of the voice behind her. Pressing an unsteady hand on her stomach, which was doing somersaults, she turned around slowly.

Gil Markum smiled at her, his face creasing with undeniable charm. One hand was in the pocket of his white trousers, and his wide shoulders strained at the fabric of the madras cotton shirt he was wearing. "Are you enjoying your vacation?"

"Yes...." Her voice wavered and died in her throat.

Gil's gaze swept over her, lingering on her firm, full breasts which the striped summer top she was wearing outlined rather than concealed. "There's something about you—besides the obvious, of course," he said.

Susan shivered at the stern simplicity of the compliment. Usually levelheaded, no one had ever affected her in this fashion before. She knew she wasn't a striking beauty and that he was merely flattering her.

"Maybe it's because you remind me of someone else," Gil said.

Susan knew she hadn't met him before coming to Lake Center. If she had, she wouldn't have forgotten.

Removing a ring of keys from his pants pocket, Gil inserted one of them into the locked door of the Lincoln. "It's a beauty, isn't it? I've only had it a few months." His hand slid over the edge of the door frame caressingly as he pulled the door open.

"It's gorgeous." Susan said, unable to hide her admiration. The word fit not only the automobile, but also its owner, she thought silently.

"Hop in. I'll take you for a ride in it."

"Oh, no. I can't...."

One dark eyebrow tilted mockingly. "Why not?"

"I...I don't have time," Susan's fingers tightened on the strap of her shoulder bag, tugged at it nervously.

"I thought you were on vacation."

"I am, but...."

His blue eyes, jaggedly cut as a glacier, seemed to cut through her defenses, leaving her speechless and permitting her no will of her own. He appeared to be toying with her, like a cat playing with a hapless field mouse. And like a mouse, she was uncertain which way to turn, which way to flee.

Taking her silence for acquiescence, Gil placed his hand on her arm and drew her along with him. The pressure of his fingers seemed to warn of the sheer futility of trying to escape. He looked down at her tauntingly as he opened the door on the passenger's side of the Lincoln. "I assure you that you'll be perfectly safe."

A flush crept over Susan's face. "I can't go with you. I have other plans...."

"We won't be gone long. I have plans for later, as well."

Feeling like a tiny boat bobbing helplessly on the crest of a tidal wave, Susan slid onto the Lincoln's soft leather seat and sank back. The instrument panel was a bewildering display of gadgets and gauges that dazzled the senses, intimidated her like the man beside her.

At the touch of the ignition, the motor leapt to life, purring softly as Gil's strong hands skillfully guided it into the street. He pushed a button and music from superb speakers filled the silence between them. The music was spellbinding, clear as a bell. It was also dangerous in conjunction with the masculinity of the man beside her. Susan shifted uneasily, edging away from him.

Gil caught her movements. "Would you prefer to listen to something else?"

"Oh, no!" she responded hastily. "This is fine."

Outside the city limits, at the touch of the accelerator, the Lincoln's powerful engine leapt forward like a jungle cat. Feeling as if she were floating on a waterbed, Susan gradually relaxed against the cushions and let the air conditioner cool her flushed body. Like the previous day, the area was blanketed with a bluish haze that made the distance seem blurred and surreal.

"This is fabulous" she murmured as the huge automobile floated over the road. The words, she knew, were inadequate.

Emitting a deep chuckle of pride, Gil grinned at her.

They proceeded several miles out of town. Then he turned the car around and headed back. When they reached Lake Sally, near the edge of town, he pulled alongside the city beach. Bright bikini-clad sunbathers lulled on the white sand. In the water, heads were bobbing up and down like corks. Laughter and screeches filled the air. Now and then a motorboat roared by, creating sweeping waves. Shrill cries and disgruntled moans sounded from the people in the water.

Gil pushed a button on his door panel and the window alongside Susan lowered. As the water rippled and gurgled against the shore, she closed her eyes and inhaled the water's freshness, felt the touch of the cooling breeze on her face. No matter how many unhappy memories returning to Lake Center, with its changing seasons and sudden summer storms, had evoked; no matter how glad she had been to leave, this was home, with the sights and smells of her childhood. There was something special, something comforting about them.

She felt the warmth of Gil's huge frame beside her, of his eyes on her. His penetrating gaze made the blood rush to her cheeks once again. To conceal it, she turned aside and stared out the window again.

"How do you like our little town?" A hint of amusement edged his tone.

Susan turned to face him. "I grew up in this little town."

"Really? Where do you live now?" When Susan told him, he asked if her parents still resided in Lake Center.

"They're both dead." She glanced at her watch. "I think I'd better be going."

She would call Kim, and check to see if she was all right. Aware of how her sister felt about Gil Markum, Susan knew she didn't dare tell Kim that she had been with him. Kim would never speak to her again.

Gil reached down and turned on the ignition. In what seemed like seconds, they were back in the parking lot.

Relief flooding through her, Susan could scarcely believe she had survived his company without acting like an unsophisticated fool. She groped for the Lincoln's door handle. "Thanks for introducing me to your car. It's beautiful."

Gil's smiled at her with enigmatic eyes. "Now that you and my car are acquainted, you and I will have to get to know each other better, too."

The invitation caught her by surprise. "I...I don't...." She wanted to tell him she was too busy to see him again, that she didn't think it was such a good idea, but her vocal cords were paralyzed.

He chuckled, his eyes crinkling in amusement at her confusion. Reaching over, he tilted her face with the tips of his fingers. "You, Susan Edwards, are a very pretty lady." His deep, grating voice made a rough caress of her name. "An enigma, but a very pretty one."

Then he was out of his car and moving around to the passenger's side. He opened the door for her and she climbed out. Fingers trembling so that opening her handbag was a struggle, she fumbled inside it for her car keys. Finally finding them, she attempted to insert the key into the Skyhawk's locked door. The key jiggled and danced so that she had difficulty finding the keyhole.

"Let me help you," Gil said from behind her. The touch of his hand on her arm burned her skin.

"No, I...." She released a jagged breath as the key slipped into the lock. Pulling open the door, she slid onto the hot car seat. As the heat penetrated the light fabric of her slacks, she shifted uneasily.

Mocking glints danced in Gil's blue eyes as his gaze held hers through the open car door. "I'll be seeing you," he said. The words were a promise, not a farewell.

Then he was inside his own car again, waiting until Susan started the engine of her Skyhawk. He had called her an enigma, a mystery. What a strange thing to say. As she drove out of the parking lot, in the side mirror, she saw his car move out of the exit on the opposite side and disappear into the line of traffic.

Stay away from that man, her head warned; *He wants to see me again,* her heart sang.

"Have you heard from Kim?" Harry asked. "Are you going out to her place?"

His call came several minutes after Susan entered the house. He had given her a key upon her arrival, and told her she was free to come and go as she pleased.

"I'm not sure," Susan answered in response to his question. "Why?"

"I've been invited to a friend's house for dinner and a game of poker. Since you're alone at the house, I'll turn down the invitation and come home."

"Don't do that. Enjoy yourself. I'll find something to do."

Harry was hesitant. "Are you sure?"

"I'm sure." Placing the receiver back on the hook, Susan vacillated several minutes, then picked it up and pressed her sister's number. After the fifth or sixth ring, Kim lifted the receiver.

"Did you get your television repaired?" Susan asked.

"The serviceman couldn't make it. He called and said he'd be here tomorrow."

"Then you're coming back to town tonight?" The words were tentative. Susan didn't want to antagonize her sister, but the thought of Kim alone in her isolated lake home made her uneasy.

"I'm staying here."

"Maybe I should come out and stay with you."

"Look, sister dear. I've been living out here by myself since Brad died. I don't need a baby sitter. I'm not a two-year old."

Taken aback by the biting words, all of Susan's childhood resentment came crashing down on her again. Kim's problem was her lousy disposition, not that she was still grief stricken because of her husband's death or that someone had knocked her around and tried to rape her. Maybe someone had good reason to be angry with her.

Susan could not forget the words of the man who had accosted her on the beach. *"Mess with me, Bitch, and you'll pay."* Those words were meant for Kim, she suspected.

She took a deep breathe in an effort to hold back her rising anger. Why had she thought she could help her sister? Why had she even bothered to try? Kim was still the spoiled, arrogant brat she had always been. All right, if that's the way she wanted it, she could solve her own problems, whatever they were. Obviously, she didn't think she had any.

"I'm sorry." There was a softening in Kim's voice as she spoke. "I didn't mean to come down on you so hard. Don't worry about me. I'll be fine. Why don't you drive out tomorrow?"

The words caught Susan by surprise. Contrition had always been foreign to Kim.

"I'll see," Susan replied, Kim's abrasiveness still heating her blood. "I don't want to bother you."

Chapter 12

"Shit!" Kim despaired as she hung up the phone. Why did Susan have to come here now? Why did she have to be playing den mother?

Kim jammed her fingers through her long, platinum hair. She had done her best to dissuade Susan short of telling her to get lost. If it hadn't been for that thing on the beach, she would probably be in LA by now, safely out of the way, reconciling with that dickhead she had been married to. Kim had pegged him as a control freak the first time she'd met him.

Her thoughts turned to what had happened to Susan on the beach. It had to have been more of a scare tactic than a threat, Kim was sure. Although she had suggested it had simply been a case of raging hormones gone awry, she hadn't believed it for a moment. She had a good idea who was responsible. No, she *knew* who was responsible.

The asshole! What did he think he was doing? The thought that the tables were being turned on her, that he might be planning to do to her what she was going to do to him if he didn't leave her alone, sent a momentary chill skittering up her spine.

He had been on her back, pressuring her lately. She had entitled him The Weasel because he was a sneaky, furtive varmint, and not to be trusted. Susan had described the man who attacked her as big and powerful. But in the dark of night and under threatening conditions, he could have appeared larger and stronger than he actually was.

Kim wished he would leave her alone. She'd about had it. Nobody was going to tell her what to do. Nobody. When she'd tripped on the steps and cut her forehead as she came up from the lake that day, the idea had flashed into her mind like a news bulletin across a television screen.

When the Weasel had first come to her and pointed out that Gil Markum was responsible for Brad's death, Kim agreed most vehemently. Even before he approached her, she had been a seething bundle of retaliatory wrath, trying to think of a way to avenge Brad's death. Playing on her emotions, encouraging her desire for vengeance, The Weasel had convinced her that stealing corporate secrets from Markum Manufacturing was the way to go. There would be no monetary pay-off for her, but she didn't want one. No amount of money would ease her pain. There was only one thing that could do that: the destruction of Gil Markum. Not quick and fiery, like Brad had died, but slow and torturously. Inch by heart wrenching inch.

Somehow the Weasel had learned that Kyle was working on a new project. Something big. She was to find out as much as she could about Markum Manufacturing's security system. The Weasel would use the information to enter the plant with no one being the wiser. He would photograph the project's plans, and sell them to Markum's competitors. She had found out that the safe where the blueprints were kept opened with a special key. She was to steal the key from the man who kept it on his person at all times, make a duplicate of it and return the original without arousing suspicion. And she had completed that part of the deal.

One night, after making love with the man she was using to achieve her goal, she had slipped out of bed and removed the key from his pants pocket. She'd made duplicates the next day. The following evening, when they'd been together again, she'd returned the key, explaining that she found it under the bed when she was vacuuming.

"I keep a second set of keys at home so I was able to open the safe," the man stated with a sigh of relief. "But thank God it was you that found these, and not someone who could convert the safe's contents to their own use."

But the key she had duplicated was of no use until entry into the main plant was accomplished. She hadn't been able to find out anything useful about the whereabouts of the security system's sensors. Falling in love with the man she was using as a pawn hadn't been in her plans either. Although it affected her intent to use him in her scheme, it hadn't affected her desire to destroy Gil Markum.

She had come up with a better way to avenge Brad's murder. It *had* been murder, not an accident. Her new plan involved nothing illegal or unethical in her mind. Nothing she could be imprisoned for if it were discovered what she was up to. But she had to get The Weasel off her back. She didn't need him anymore. He wouldn't be happy about that. He was expecting to get his scrawny paws on some big bucks. Somehow, she had to convince him that they should forget the whole thing, that she couldn't find out anything more about the security system. It would be too risky for The Weasel to break in without any knowledge of where the sensors were or how to avoid them. He wasn't about to take any risks himself.

Kyle was Gil Markum's Achilles heel, the one thing he cared about more than money or power. If Gil were to lose his son, it would mean no more string-pulling, no more super big contracts. If Kim had found out anything worthwhile, it had been that Markum Manufacturing received its most profitable business contracts with the help of Marisa's father. If Gil lost the help of his son's talent and expertise and the political pull of that son's father-in-law, Markum Manufacturing would lose the major share of its business.

Gil had taken away her life's blood; she would take away his. She was using different tactics to bring that about than she had first planned to, but, hopefully, they would attain the same results.

Kim tensed as the shrill ringing of the telephone cut into the room like a steel-edged saber.

Was Susan calling back? No, she had been pissed after their phone conversation. Oh, she might want to call back, but her pride wouldn't let her. Or was it another crank call like the ones she'd been receiving in the past month or so? Her blood sizzling, Kim wondered why the caller didn't spit it out instead of hiding in the bushes, trying to intimidate her. Didn't they know she didn't scare easily?

Or was it the Weasel? Now that she had come to care about the man they had been using in their plans, The Weasel had a hold on her. He was using it for all it was worth to get what he wanted. He made a living being devious, playing dirty. He had told her he was in need of 'funds', and he sensed her growing reluctance to help him get them.

Slowly, apprehension holding back her hand, Kim reached for the phone. "Hello...?"

"Hello, darling. I miss you."

Kim released a deep sigh of relief. "I've missed you, too," she said softly.

"Do you still have company?"

"Not now. Susan won't be back until tomorrow."

"I'm coming out. I love you. See you in five minutes."

Chapter 13

Harry's meager supply of reading material left a great deal to be desired. Not one for summer re-runs on television, Susan replaced a dog-eared paperback on the coffee table and wondered what she would do with the long evening that stretched before her. The ringing of the telephone cut into her dilemma.

"Just checking to see if you went out to Kim's place," Reid said.

"She doesn't exactly appreciate my concern or my company."

"Had a sibling fight, did you?"

"I love my sister, but sometimes I'd like to strangle her."

Reid chortled. "Been there. I have two brothers. So what are you up to now?"

"I'm at loose ends. Harry is spending the evening with friends. If I can find something worth reading, I'll probably curl up on the couch with a book. But westerns and James Bond don't exactly turn me on."

There was a pause on Reid's end of the line. "Since I'm not working tonight, why don't we have dinner together...unless you'd rather curl up with Louie Lamour...."

Susan was taken aback by the invitation. After what had happened on the beach, spending the evening alone in a strange house made her uneasy. Going out to dinner, even if it was with a man she didn't especially like, sounded better than the gunfight at the OK corral.

Since the breakup of her marriage, she'd had a tendency to avoid male companionship. Reid seemed like a safe candidate for her maiden journey. There was little chance of anything, perhaps even friendship, developing between them. Abrasive and bitter, he was haunted by the memories of his wife. He was as consumed by them as Kim was consumed by the loss of Brad.

"Maybe, between the two of us, we can come up with something that's been overlooked in your sister's case," Reid said.

Susan was grateful for his dedication, but she didn't want to think about Kim or her troubles. She wanted to laugh and joke and stuff herself with food, to forget why she had come here.

Reid arrived an hour later. Out of uniform, he looked like a different man. His beige slacks were neatly creased, and the white cotton shirt he wore was open at the neckline disclosing a bristle of chest hair. During his high school years, his rugged handsomeness and daredevil manner had had all the girls fantasizing about him. Now, tempered by age and misfortune, his bold, reckless demeanor was no longer evident. But his attractiveness remained, marred only slightly by the lines etched in his face.

His gaze took in her sleeveless lavender dress and the frosty white necklace around her neck. "You look very nice."

Surprised by the compliment, Susan's cheeks warmed. "Thank you."

"I apologize for the wheels, but a bachelor like me only needs one vehicle," he said as he opened the door of his black Jeep Cherokee for her. "I prefer a four-wheel drive for the winters we have around here. It helps keep me on the road. After living in Arizona for so long, I've discovered I've forgotten how to drive on ice and snow."

Susan was glad the evening was starting off on a casual, friendlier note.

As she glanced about the Jeep, she wasn't overwhelmed like she'd been in Gil's Lincoln Continental. The interior of the Cherokee showed definite signs of wear, but it was spick and span. The dash gleamed in the light of the evening sun. The seat cushions had softened from use, but a faint scent of their leather fabric still lingered.

Reid took her to a small supper club several miles outside of Lake Center. Capable of seating fifty or sixty people, somehow the restaurant appeared to seat half that number. It had the quietly understated atmosphere of a tavern, a low ceiling crossed with dark-varnished beams. The tables were draped in crisp white linen and set with silverware. Pulling the small vase in the center of the table closer, Susan inhaled the sweet aroma of the single rose it held and twisted the curling sprigs of ivy surrounding the flower around the end of her finger. She was glad Reid hadn't taken her to The Bayside where the chance existed that they might run into Gil Markum.

As they waited for their meal to be served, Susan and Reid sipped the wine they had ordered and engaged in light conversation. The warm glow of the subdued lighting softened the lines around his mouth and nose and deeply set eyes, giving him a gentler, more amicable appearance.

Whenever the conversation turned to the events that had been taking place at Kim's place, Susan steered it away, and they talked about movies, sports and politics. They discovered their likes were similar. Their salads were large and crisp, and when the Chicken Parmigiana they'd both ordered was served, it was delicious.

"How long have you been in police work?" Susan asked as she speared a forkful of lettuce.

"I enrolled at the police academy shortly after Linda and I moved to Phoenix," Reid answered. "As soon as I finished, I went to work for their police department."

"Why did you decide on a career in law enforcement? If my memory serves me correctly, you were in more than one skirmish as a teenager." Admittedly, his youthful antics had been more prankish than criminal—getting into fights, driving too fast or without a license, trying to outrun the cops to avoid a ticket.

"I guess I grew up and decided to turn my energy on outwitting the bad guys instead of acting like one." Pausing, with a crooked smile, he added, "I have the feeling you aren't especially impressed with my capabilities."

Color deepened on Susan's cheeks. "I'm sorry if I gave you that idea." She paused, then confessed, "I did have doubts at first, but now...."

Her embarrassment seemed to amuse him. "What changed your mind? I doubt if it was my charming bedside manner. Was it my jeep or the Chicken Parmigiana?"

Susan laughed. "More likely it's the wine I've been drinking. Wine makes me do strange things sometime."

His mouth curving in a small smile, Reid lifted his glass in a salute. "Hopefully not too strange." Sobering, he urged, "Tell me about your ex-husband. What's he like?"

Susan was reflective for a moment. "He's charming. Attractive. Ambitious...."

"And?" Reid waited, his gaze fixed on her face.

"And he has the tendency to dominate everyone around him. He didn't want me to wear anything colorful or in the least way provocative. Naturally, I wanted to please him." By bowing to Mark's wishes, she had thought she could make him love her more. "After the divorce, I went wild. I bought splashy reds and chic blacks, dresses with low necklines and slits up the leg. Mark hated lavender. I bought this outfit, and I've worn it until it's almost threadbare. I probably look horrible in it, but *I* made the decision to buy it. *I* made the decision to wear it."

"Low necklines and slits up the legs doesn't sound like you at all," Reid said.

"They aren't," Susan admitted with a little laugh. "My acts of defiance have been limited, however. Beyond purchasing a new wardrobe, I haven't been quite sure how to get on with my life."

"What do you want out of life?" Reid's gaze was intent on her face.

Susan sipped her wine, swirled it around in the glass. "Nothing as noble as saving the world or as ambitious as setting it on fire. Mostly, I want to be a wife, to have a house in the country with a couple of kids and a dog running around." She wanted the love and affection she had been denied while she was growing up. She wanted to be part of a family, to be thought of as an equal partner, not a subservient one.

"Are you going to give your ex-husband another chance to give you those things?" Reid asked.

No matter what was happening to her inside, she had always tried to think things through, to maintain an outward calm. She'd learned that defense over the years, to remain detached and impervious. Unlike the headstrong Kim, she usually tested the waters before jumping in—until she'd met Mark. Then she had dove in headfirst.

"Mark says he's changed. The fact is," she conceded, "he was usually right about everything."

Reid's mouth twisted into a wry smile. "Makes you want to punch someone like that in the nose, doesn't it?'

"There were times," Susan confessed. Welcoming his more amicable, less gruff, abrupt demeanor, she gave him an appreciative smile.

"You can't learn from your mistakes if you aren't allowed to make any." He took a long, slow drink of wine. Sometimes it's difficult to revive a relationship, especially if it wasn't what you expected it to be in the first place."

"I remind myself of that." Surprised at the unexpected communication that had blossomed between them, Susan forgot about the earlier hostility that had existed between them. Usually a private person, she discovered herself talking about her childhood and her life with her father and stepmother.

"Does your step-mother still live in Lake Center?" Reid asked.

"She sold the house and left town shortly after my father died, taking the proceeds with her. I really didn't care. The house wasn't worth much. It wasn't kept up or the necessary repairs made on it. My father wasted his paycheck and his health on booze."

"Sounds like you had a great childhood."

As a child, in an effort to escape from the cold, uncaring world she'd found herself thrust into after the death of her mother, she had spent many lonely hours in the confines of her bedroom. She'd used her imagination to see through the walls, to set her mind adrift. *Tomorrow will be different,* she'd told herself over and over.

She was still waiting for tomorrow to arrive.

"I tried to stay out of the way as much as possible," Susan reflected soberly. "I spent a great deal of time in my room daydreaming that someday someone would come along and take me away from all of that."

"Someone like Mark."

"I suppose so." In retrospect, Susan realized she had been looking a little too hard, had been too willing to make concessions. Oh, Mark had given her what her father had not—a sense of security, of belonging to someone, but she had learned it wasn't enough, that she needed an identity, too.

"On our way to the supermarket yesterday, Kim and I drove past the house I grew up in. Although it's been remodeled, the sight of it brought back a lot of memories."

"I know what you mean. Memories have a habit of coming back."

Reid was, suddenly, remote. Inaccessible. He was lonely too, Susan saw, with only bitterness and an empty heart to keep him company.

"Would you like to talk about it?" she asked quietly.

He had never talked about it with anyone. Deputy sheriffs were tough. Strong. They dealt with crime, tried to make the world a safer place to live. They didn't talk about personal problems. They didn't talk about how much they hurt when they lost someone they loved. They kept it to themselves. No one had ever said, 'Would you like to talk about it?'

Quietly, he talked about the cancer. About seeing Linda die a little each day until she was nothing but dull, pain-filled eyes and fragile bones, and not being able to do a damned thing about it.

"After she passed away, I kept seeing her everywhere. In the kitchen, in the bedroom, on the patio with my "Kiss the Cook" apron wrapped around her waist twice. How the scent of her favorite perfume lingered in the bedroom months after she was gone." His voice mirrored the pain that the memory had revived. Whenever he caught the scent of White Shoulders on another woman, memories of Linda twisted his heart into knots.

"It's part of the reason I came back here," he went on, his eyes darkening in reflection. "It makes it a little easier. At least I don't keep seeing her every time I turn around. Oh, I see the young girl I dated, the places where we used to go when we were young, but I don't see the woman Linda became or the woman I held in my arms and shared a home with. The woman I made love to at night."

"I know," Susan empathized quietly. "Mark didn't die, but our marriage did. Your pain will lessen in time. But it takes longer than anyone says it will."

His family and friends had told him the pain would ease, too. That he had to get on with his life. Oh, the memories had faded a little around the edges, but he would never forget Linda. There had never been anyone else for him. He doubted if there ever would be.

"While the marriages of a lot of our friends were crumbling around them, Linda and I had a wonderful marriage," he said, unable to keep the bitterness out of his voice. "But it was snatched away, as if we weren't supposed to be happy. I've never been able to understand it; it doesn't seem fair. But who the hell ever said life was fair?"

His angry words seemed to fill the room the way they filled his heart. Every nook and corner. Every empty space.

He pulled himself erect in his chair and cleared his throat. "I'm sorry. I didn't ask you to have dinner with me so I could cry on your shoulder. I asked you out because I thought we could talk about what's been going on at your sister's place. Maybe get some extra input...."

"I don't want to talk about Kim's problems," Susan confessed. "My mind needs a break. I haven't thought of much else since Harry called me. How can you help someone who doesn't want your help?" She brushed back the soft fringe of bangs on her brow.

The spat she'd had with her sister must have been a doozy, Reid determined. Susan was still pissed. She had clearly endured more than her share of heartbreak and disappointment. Yet she hadn't gone off the deep end like her sister had. There was a warmth, a compassion inside Susan, an inner strength that he admired. It wasn't easy to keep smiling when you'd been kicked in the teeth. She seemed determined to help her sister. On the other hand, Kim was so wrapped up in herself and her problems—whatever they were—that she was blind to Susan's wants and needs.

He wondered why the Hastings' case was so important to him that he took it home with him, had taken it out to dinner with him tonight. Law officers were supposed to be objective. They weren't supposed to become involved in the personal aspects of a crime. He justified his actions by telling himself it was natural for him to want to find out what was going on. As a deputy sheriff, it was his job to solve crimes and catch criminals, no matter who they were.

Kim was obviously having difficulty dealing with her husband's death. There was anger and bitterness burning inside her. He understood that part all too well.

But there was something else, too. She was a ticking time bomb, ready to explode.

Chapter 14

▼

"Miss Edwards?" the voice on the phone wanted to know.

Susan recognized Esther Helgeson's thick, Scandinavian brogue. "Good morning, Esther."

"I called your sister's place a few minutes ago, and she gave me this number. As a matter of fact, I woke her up. She didn't sound too happy about that."

Susan waited, her stomach muscles tightening.

"I talked to my grandson," the older woman continued. "Remember, you were wondering if he'd seen or heard anything the day your sister was beaten up?"

Susan's heart skipped a beat. "Yes...."

"Danny said the day he was here he saw a shiny red sports car parked in Kim's driveway when he and Butch were chasin' squirrels in the woods near her house."

A thief with a sports car? Susan thought in dismay. It was highly unlikely. Danny must have his days mixed up.

"How old is your grandson, Esther?" Susan asked.

"He's six. He's in the first grade."

"Is he sure it was a sports car that he saw?"

"That boy's as smart as a whip. If he says he saw a red sports car, that's what it was. He said it was a Corvette, just like the one his best friend's uncle has."

Esther Helgeson's grandson might be as smart as a whip, Susan thought. He also had an active imagination, too active to be for real. He was undoubtedly making it up, seeing himself as a celebrity.

Moments after Susan thanked Esther for the information and placed the phone on its cradle, it rang again, startling her.

"Did Esther Helgeson call you?" Kim asked. "What did she want?"

Susan searched her mind for a response that wouldn't incriminate her and yet satisfy Kim's curiosity. "She told me that her grandson is visiting her...."

"Why should she bother to do that? Stop playing detective, Sue." There was a pause, and then Kim said, "I called to tell you things have changed. I have something to do today. You'll have to come out tomorrow instead."

A frown creased Susan's brow. "Are you all right?"

"Of course I'm all right. See you tomorrow, okay? We'll go swimming again, have a picnic on the beach." There was a weighty pause, and then Kim spoke again. "Sorry I was such a bitch yesterday."

Susan was taken aback. It wasn't like Kim to apologize for anything, unheard of for her to repeat an apology. Kim usually defended her actions, right or wrong. Unlike her sister, Susan didn't like to argue or fight. As a child, whenever her father and stepmother launched into one of their many battles, she had covered her ears and fled into her bedroom.

"Has the TV repairman been out yet?" Susan asked.

"Not yet," Kim replied. "If he doesn't come today, he'll be here tomorrow."

After hanging up from the conversation with Kim, Susan called the newspaper office and asked Harry if he were free for lunch.

"Has Kim said any more about the robbery attempt at her place? About being knocked around?" he asked as he and Susan sat across from each other in Miller's Cafe.

"She refuses to talk about it."

"What about that thing that happened to you on the beach?"

Since Kim had been assaulted herself, Susan found her sister's casual dismissal of the matter difficult to understand. Susan had been unable to close her eyes without reliving what had happened. Without seeing the black, faceless menace coming at her, hearing the thud of his footfall in the sand, feeling his huge fingers tightening around her throat. "Kim thinks it was some weirdo walking along the beach who, when he saw me, had an inexplicable urge to attack me."

Harry chortled. "I don't buy that. Sorry I dragged you into this, Suzy."

Susan placed her hand atop his gnarled, veined one. "You were concerned about Kim."

"For all the good it does!"

"I'll be all right," Susan assured him. "Kim says she can take care of herself. She has a gun...."

"A gun!" Harry's faded blue eyes widened in horror behind his wire-rimmed glasses.

"She says she'll use it if she has to."

Harry took a deep breath, then released it slowly. "After what's happened out there, I suppose havin' a gun isn't such a bad idea. But the thought of her needin' one...." He broke off, shaking his head in disbelief.

"I heard you come home last night," he went on after a long moment.

"Reid Elison asked me to have dinner with him."

Harry's shaggy brows arched. "So you two are hittin' it off better?"

"I understand him a little better." The animosity between them had softened over dinner, making them more at ease with each other. It was as if, having endured deep losses, they had become, momentarily at least, kindred spirits.

After lunching with Harry, Susan made her way to her car that she had parked in the lot behind the cafe again. Heat rose from the concrete, striking her face like a burst from a blast furnace. Halting beside her Skyhawk, she brushed back a wisp of hair that clung to her cheek. As she fumbled in her handbag for the car keys, a familiar white automobile eased into the space alongside her. She stepped closer to her own vehicle.

A smiling Gil Markum opened the door of his luxury automobile and climbed out. "We meet again. It must be karma."

Susan flushed as his eyes flickered over her, taking in her clingy tank top and white shorts. Standing close to the poised, confident tycoon with the snowy white hair and bronzed, youthful face, filled her with conflicting emotions; feelings of both attraction toward him and a sense of apprehension. For a moment, she wanted to run as fast and as far as her legs could carry her. The problem was her knees felt as if they were about to buckle beneath her.

"How about you and I going for a swim?" Gil asked. The blue and white striped shirt he was wearing made him appear broader and larger than she remembered him to be.

"A swim?" she repeated. She shifted nervously as he peered at her with his inscrutable blue eyes. His parting words after she had gone on the memorable ride with him in his Lincoln had been, 'Now that you and my car are acquainted, you and I will have to get to know each other, too.' Those words had remained imprinted on her mind, had often intruded on her thoughts and heated her blood.

"If you don't want to go for a swim, perhaps we could have dinner together tonight." Gil's smile and the look in his eyes was as much of a challenge as an invitation.

"I don't know...." Desperately, she searched her mind for a plausible excuse to decline his invitation.

His eyes held hers, daring her rejection. "The pool at my place awaits us. We'll have dinner afterwards."

"I don't have a swim suit with me."

"I'm sure there's an extra one in the bath house." He placed one hand on her elbow, then opened the door on the passenger's side of his luxury car. His touch, confident and sure, told her that he was a man used to getting his way with women.

Susan held back. "What about my car?"

"I'll bring you back here…safe and sound," he promised mockingly. As his piercing gaze held hers, she felt like a novice walking a high wire without a net. And she desperately needed a net, she feared.

Why was he so interested in her? What did he see in her? There were many women more beautiful, more interesting than she was. *"There's only one way to find out,"* an inner voice whispered. Standing beside her like a jungle animal, muscles rippling under deeply tanned skin, he took her breath away. If she refused him, sheer instinct told her he would consider her more of a challenge, and be more determined. She knew it was insane to get involved with this man. Yet she didn't want to say no to his invitation.

On the drive out to his place, Gil pointed out changes in the area and told her of the impending plans he had for Lake Center. There was a new beachfront, an all-season complex, and a lakeside condominium. As she listened to him, his low, grating voice seemed to vibrate with an underlying sensuality. He was, she discovered, quick witted and knowledgeable on a great number of subjects. Politics. Travel. Finance. He was an active participant in sports as well as an avid fan. He liked to fish and hunt, especially big game. He swam, golfed, and went scuba diving in the Caribbean.

"Are you staying at a resort or with friends or relatives while you're in town?" The breeze coming through the open car window lifted his thick thatch of white hair with light fingers.

"I'm sort of hopping back and forth," Susan explained. "Sometimes I'm at my uncle's place. Sometimes I'm at the lake."

"How long have your parents been gone?"

"My mother died when I was a child, my father several years ago. I have a sister." What would he think if he knew her sister considered him a murderer?

"How do you like living in Lake Center?" The question was inane, but Susan knew she must steer the conversation to safer grounds.

"I make a point of making the best of things wherever I am. I located here because this town afforded me a good business climate, and there was an adequate work force. I've had to build on to the plant since I opened it five years ago. Of course, a good deal of its success must be attributed to my son." Gil's countenance was aglow with pride. "He's working on a new concept now that will revolutionize the auto industry and make millions."

"Do you know my son? I believe you saw his wife at The Bayside the other night, didn't you? Now, as far as how I like living in Lake Center...." A smile curved his mouth. "I'm finding it much more interesting than I did a few days ago."

Once again, Susan was caught up by the magnetism of the man beside her. Never, in her wildest dreams, had she met anyone like him. She had the scary feeling that a force had been unleashed that could take control of her life if she allowed it to. To have someone control her life again was something she neither needed nor wanted.

Warning bells and lights were going off inside her like a tilted pinball machine. Still, she was intrigued by him, fascinated and drawn to the danger with an overwhelming force.

Gil turned into a tree-lined driveway. "Here we are,"

A contrast of rough-hewn granite and polished surfaces like its owner, his house was constructed mainly of stone and glass, and built into the side of the cliff overlooking the lake. A vast, beautifully manicured lawn and a dense grove of conifers and hardwood trees surrounded it. To one side was a tennis court, on the other, a patio containing a huge umbrella-shaded wrought iron table and four chairs. Adjoining the back of the house was a magnificent kidney-shaped swimming pool with azure tile, giving the water in it an illusion of a miniature sea.

"It's beautiful," a wide-eyed Susan marveled.

Taking her arm, Gil led her into a large living room. Motioning for her to sit on a black, soft-leathered sofa, he moved over to a mahogany bar. "Can I get you something to drink?"

"A wine cooler is fine if you have it," Susan replied, glancing about the room in awe.

She saw heavy, rich-grained furniture arranged attractively on a plush gray carpet; textured gray drapery at the windows. Large brass lamps and splashes of color in the sofa pillows and the paintings on the wall accented the simplicity of the room. Above a huge, graystone fireplace, the glassy yellow eyes in a mounted tiger's head glared down at her. Its jaws were spread wide, as if it were about to devour someone.

Walking back from the far side of the room where he had mixed himself a drink at the bar, Gil handed her a glass of wine cooler. He sat down beside her, a scotch and water in his hand. On his way over to the bar, he had switched on the stereo, and the music playing from it wrapped itself softly around them. Susan felt light-headed without having had a drop to drink. Her pulse was in overdrive. She wished she could slow it down, that her mind would listen when she told it to do so, but her libido refused to obey. Her hands were clammy as she clutched her glass of wine. What was she doing in this house with this man? She must be out of her mind to have come here. This place—and this man—were a whole different world.

They chatted for a brief time, but whenever Gil attempted to draw her out about her personal life, she steered the conversation to other things.

"What a mysterious lady you are," he said as he studied her face with searching eyes.

The words brought a smile to Susan's face. "Don't I wish. There's nothing interesting to tell. I'm just plain Susan Edwards."

"Plain Susan Edwards? I don't think so. Don't underrate yourself." He paused a moment. "You remind me of someone. It's been driving me crazy ever since I first met you."

That she could have such an effect on a man amused her, but it was flattering, too. It certainly was an ego booster after the demise of her marriage, of living with a man impossible to please.

Hands trembling slightly, she placed her wineglass on the coffee table. "Maybe we'd better go for that swim."

"That is what we came here to do, isn't it?" Gil said with a grin. "I'll show you to the bath house. You'll find a swim suit there—if you insist on wearing one." His eyes danced mischievously.

She flushed. "I insist."

Minutes later, as she walked across the stone terrace in a brief white bikini, Susan shaded her eyes from the glare of the afternoon sunlight and peered across the lake to the area where her sister's house was located. What was Kim doing that she had turned her away, told her to come out tomorrow? Was she seeing the person who had called her the other day, the person she had gone to meet? Had it been a friend? A lover? By the way Kim had been acting, because of her love for her deceased husband, it was highly unlikely she was having an affair with someone.

From where he stood a short distance away dressed in a pair of spandex trunks, Susan felt Gil's eyes traveling appraisingly over her scantily clad body, down her long legs. A wash of telltale color flooded over her face once again. Turning away, she took several steps and dove headlong into the pool. Gil followed behind her.

Side by side, they swam the length of the pool numerous times, splashed in the water playfully. Then they climbed out and sat down near the edge of the pool. In the brightness of the late afternoon sun, Gil's muscular, sun-bronzed body glistened with droplets of water. His thick shock of hair was plastered to his head. From his position alongside Susan, he leaned over and gently brushed back a stray strand of dripping hair from her temple. She was leaning back on her hands, and as he looked down into her eyes, she knew he was going to kiss her. She felt the roughness of his fingers as they moved to probe the thickness of her wet hair, as they slid down her neck and shoulders. His head lowered. Hovered.

When his mouth moved down to press against hers, his kiss was exactly as she had known it would be. Hungry. Overpowering. She arched her body away from him, tried to escape his grasp. As his lips moved down her throat, over the swell of her breasts, she felt as if she were sliding under a slow-moving wave; as if she were back in the pool again, being drawn into its silky, shimmering water. Her mind went blank as her pulse leapt to a roar in her spinning head. She saw the arousal in his eyes as he looked at her, felt that basic need stir inside herself.

She heard a moan, low and deep, and was unsure if it were Gil or herself.

She drew back, let out a shaky breath. She lifted a hand to hold him away. "No…I don't think we should…."

"Why not?" Gil's voice was husky with emotion, yet edged with a teasing quality.

She had never done anything impulsive or risky in her life. Foolish and unwitting, perhaps. Even stupid at times. But not risky or dangerous, as she knew this was. She had slid through the layers of life, experiencing few memorable moments or leaving little evidence that she had been there. She drew in another long breath, and pushed up the strap of her swimsuit that he had slid off her shoulder. "This is crazy…"

His laughter was husky. "What's wrong with being a little crazy once in a while?" He pulled her against him again. As his bare flesh pressed against hers, her breath caught. *'Can't. Shouldn't,'* she thought, but there was no strength in her arms as they pressed against his broad chest.

One more kiss, she told herself. Then she would insist that he take her home. He was every bit as potent as she had expected he would be;

a man who got what he wanted. And that he wanted her was an aphrodisiac which made her breath quicken and her heart pound. Helplessly, need ruled over mind and blood roared over reason, and she gave in to the moment's madness. Her nails dug into hard firmness of his bare shoulders. His chest was broad and hairy, his flesh searing against her water-cooled body. His arms were strong and muscular as they held her against him.

His next kiss was ravenous. Tongues tangled. Teeth nipped. The deep moan that sounded in his throat went straight to her head like hot brandy. Slowly, her arms moved up to wind around his neck. His hands were everywhere. Touching. Stroking. Sliding. Large rough fingers against smooth, bare skin. Clever fingers. Fingers experienced at knowing how to evoke pleasure. She moaned softly. Pressed against him.

"No." She pushed him away again, her heart thundering inside her. Tilting her chin in defiance, she struggled to her feet. "I'm going to change." It was better to play it safe than to be stupid. And giving in to this man would definitely be a stupid move on her part.

Inside the bathhouse, the swimsuit clung tightly to her flushed skin and she swore as she tugged at it. She had to get out of here before she became the victim of her own desires. When she came out of the bathhouse a few minutes later dressed in her shorts and tank top, she found Gil, fully clothed too, and standing beside the pool.

"I can't let you leave without giving you a tour of the place," he said, as if nothing had happened between them.

In spite of her protests, he took hold of her arm. As he gave her a tour of the house and the beautifully landscaped grounds, making humorous comments from time to time, his voice curled around her, melting her bones and her resolve. The pictures on the paneled walls of his study spoke of African safaris and deep-sea fishing. The house's decor exuded masculinity and expensive taste, but she neither saw nor absorbed little of it. It was as if she were disembodied, hovering above, looking down on Gil and the woman he was walking arm in arm with, smiling at.

A half-hour later, they were seated at the wrought iron table on the patio, complete with an umbrella. In the center of the table was an ice bucket with a bottle of white wine nestling in a bed of chipped ice, along with two wine goblets on a silver tray. Removing the sunglasses he had put on before their walk around the grounds, he filled the goblets from the bottle and handed her one of them.

Her eyes squinting against the brightness of the sun, she smiled at him. "This," she nodded toward the ice bucket and the wine, "just happened to be waiting, as if by magic, to quench our thirst?"

He grinned at her. "My housekeeper is well trained. That sometimes requires a magical touch." He tapped his goblet to Susan's.

"Very good," she murmured after taking a sip of the smooth, refreshing liquid.

"It's a dry Sancerre." He flashed her a smile, warm, charming and flirtatious. "You strike me as a woman who appreciates a fine wine."

She scarcely knew the difference between a 'fine dry Sancerre' and a decent Chablis. It was true, Susan thought, that she found him irresistible. Whether he was poison or the man of her dreams didn't seem to matter. She was here with him and she didn't want to wake up.

As they sat in the shade sipping their drinks, his voice curled around her hypnotically. The heat of the man beside her, and the sun and the wine bubbling in her veins warmed her, melted her bones and her will. Giving into the moment was effortless, she saw as she took another sip from her goblet. Awakening afterwards, she was afraid, could prove to be devastating. Her first instinct was to wait and see, but she sensed she would regret those actions.

Placing the goblet on the table, she rose to her feet. "I'd better go…"

"You're like a doe, ready to run at the slightest sign of danger," Gil accused as stood up. He spread his hands face-up. "See—no weapons. I'm no threat to you. You don't have to run away from me."

He had many weapons, she thought. Charm. Good looks. Wealth. A sensual voice and a smile that drew her to him like a fly into a spider web.

"You can't leave yet," he said. "My invitation was for a swim and dinner, remember? And dinner awaits us. There's nothing more devastating than having a candlelight dinner with an empty chair across from you."

Before she could protest, he placed his hand on her waist, and steered her into the house and the dining room.

A vase filled with fresh flowers sat in the center of an oak pedestal table set with silver and gold edged china. Lighted candles flickered, casting dancing patterns on the lace tablecloth. Soft music from the stereo floated out around them as he pulled out a chair for her.

"Crab salad a`la Markum," he said, lifting the cover off a large silver tray after they both were seated. A delicious aroma wafted out, filling Susan's nostrils and stirring her taste buds.

"Is your magical chef responsible for this, too?" she asked as he placed a spoonful of salad on her plate.

"I've been known to grill a steak now and then, but I have to give my housekeeper credit for this."

Susan took a forkful of the salad, followed it with a sip of wine. "I imagine you keep her busy. I'm sure you wine and dine female guests here all the time."

He looked into her eyes, his own glinting teasingly. "I've been known to do that on occasion, but you're by far the most intriguing woman I've had in my clutches in a long time."

She picked up her wineglass, a purely defensive gesture. "That sounds ominous."

He grinned in amusement, clearly enjoying her discomposure.

She had come to Lake Center to help and befriend her sister, Susan thought as she set down her glass and reached for a slice of French bread. But here she was enjoying an intimate candlelight dinner with the man Kim hated and was plotting vengeance against. Common sense vied with desire and instinct and told her she shouldn't be here, that it was madness.

When they finished dinner, she stood up and pushed back her chair. "I don't mean to be ungracious, but I do have to go."

Gil rose to his feet. "You know you really don't want to."

"Yes…I…."

Then he was pulling her into his arms, tilting her head. "Look into my eyes and tell me that you want to leave."

She was helpless and limp in his arms, unable to meet his gaze. She knew, if she stayed here another minute, it would only complicate her already convoluted life.

"You can't, can you?" There was triumph in his voice as he spoke. Lowering his head, he kissed her.

His mouth was hot and hard on hers. His huge frame pressed against her so that, as the heat and need poured out, she couldn't tell if it came from him or from herself. How easy it was to ignore the rules, to give in to her desire. She couldn't believe that she, Miss Mouse, was standing here, being kissed by this wealthy, gorgeous man who could have any woman in the world.

She couldn't, didn't want to stop him. This kind of raw, powerful need was fascinating and foreign to her. It left her defenseless and confused. Her mouth met his, just as insatiable as his. The kiss roughened, bordered on pain as his teeth scraped and nipped. She clutched his shoulders, gasping for breath, quaking with desire as his skillful mouth moved alongside her neck and sent wild chills over her skin.

She could feel his arousal as she leaned into him. She shivered as his huge hands moved over her, claiming her breasts, sliding down to her buttocks to pull her closer. She gripped his shoulders to steady herself.

As she pressed against him, she envisioned what it would feel like to let him make love to her. It would be hot. Fiery. All consuming. She tried to think, to consider the consequences of that happening, but her needs, her desire overpowered logic. Never had she experienced such primal need.

His fingers reached under her tank top, stroked the bare skin, and began to tug at the snaps of her bra.

"*People like us don't play in Markum's ball park,*" Harry had said.

She pulled back, out of Gil's arms. Regret and distress surged over her. How could she have allowed this to go so far?

She wasn't going to have a one-night stand with a man who sprinkled girls like her on his cereal for breakfast. She wasn't going to give in to his desires, no matter how tempted she was, to relinquish bits and pieces of herself like spoils in what she was sure would be another waived battle. Men like Gil Markum didn't make commitments to the Susan Edwards in the world.

"Please take me home."

His eyes boring challengingly into hers, Gil waited for her to weaken. When she didn't waver, his arms dropped to his side. "All right, if you insist, but it's early…"

No, it was late. It had almost been <u>too</u> late.

Chapter 15

▼

"What in the world are you doing out in the boonies?" Mark wanted to know. "I've called several times, but I haven't been able to get hold of you."

Before she'd left St. Paul, Susan had phoned his office to inform him she was going to spend a few days in Lake Center before flying to Los Angeles. He had been out so she had left a message where she could be reached.

"I've been moving around quite a bit," she explained now. "I came here to see Kim. She's been having a rough time since Brad's death. I was on my way out to her place just now when the phone rang."

"I didn't know you and Kim were that close."

"She's my sister. The only family I have."

"When are you coming out to LA?"

Susan hesitated. "I'm not sure."

"What do you mean you're not sure?" Mark wanted to know. "Kim has always been able to take care of herself. I'm sure she's still capable of doing so." Susan could almost see the frown of disapproval on his brow.

"Kim has changed. She seems lost...she's very bitter...."

"I've changed my schedule so we can spend time together when you arrive," Mark said. "If you don't get here pretty soon, I'll have to change it again."

"I'm sorry if I'm messing up your schedule," Susan apologized. "But I can't give you a definite time. I'll call you."

"I need something more concrete than that."

Disappointed by his insensitivity and his casual dismissal of her concerns for her sister, Susan felt her irritation stirring. "I can't promise anything more than if I decide to come to Los Angeles, I'll give you a call." She spoke slowly, emphasizing the words.

"What's going on with you, Susan?" he wanted to know.

"Kim needs someone. Except for Harry, I'm the only family she has."

"Doesn't the two of us trying again mean anything to you?" he asked.

"Of course," she replied quickly. "But my sister needs me."

When Susan hung up the phone a few minutes later, she was proud of herself for standing up to Mark. For months, like a child holding a broken doll in its hand, wanting it to be back together the way it once had been, she had waited, wondered if there was a chance that they could work out things. But she had made up her mind that she wouldn't be swayed by his demands or intimidating ways. She was determined not to make that mistake again.

Since their divorce, she had avoided relationships that could remotely be construed as or would lead to closeness. Yet last night, she had found herself drowning in Gil's arms, wanting to succumb to his wishes. Thank God she had come to her senses before she had lost it entirely. How long would she be able to hold onto her new found courage? If she and Gil were together again under similar circumstances, would she be able to resist? Did she want to?

Last night, after Gil brought her back to the parking lot where she had left her Skyhawk, he had looked down at her in the yellow glow of the light from the street lamps. "This is goodnight, but not goodbye," he said, kissing her lightly on the cheek. "There will be another time. I don't give up easily."

Thank God she'd had the strength to insist that he take her home. And minutes ago, she had stood up to Mark. Admittedly, she hadn't won the battle yet, only a couple of skirmishes, but there was hope for her. Swinging the strap of her handbag over her shoulder, she headed for the door.

When there was no response to a press on Kim's doorbell, Susan stood on the doorstep fidgeting uneasily. Where was her sister at this time of the morning? Still in bed? The afternoon of her arrival, she had found Kim dressed in a robe and looking as if she had just gotten up.

Susan felt a chill, like an ice scraper along her spine. What if....

The wild drumming of a woodpecker hunting breakfast echoed through the still air, matching the frantic beat of her heart,

Then the door opened and Kim stood in the entrance. Her unbelted, robe gaped open in the front revealing a short, sheer blue nightie. Her long, platinum hair was in disarray about her fine-featured face. She stared in confusion, her brows knitted. "What are you doing here?" Removing her hand from the doorknob, she pulled her robe closer around her.

Susan frowned. "You asked me to come out this morning, remember?"

Kim shoved back her hair with a nervous gesture. "Oh, yes…but I wasn't expecting you this early."

As the door eased open a trifle more, behind her sister, Susan noticed a man's suit coat draped over the back of a chair. Judging by Kim's state of dress and her obvious discomfort, she'd had an overnight guest.

Susan blinked in bewilderment. What was going on? Hours ago Kim had been despondent and embittered. She had vowed to avenge Brad's death, had professed an undying love for him. Now her face was flushed and her lips bruised, as if from excessive kissing.

"Why don't you come back this afternoon…around four?" Kim suggested. "I'll take you out to dinner."

Susan's irritation rose at the idea that she was being put off again. It seemed as if she was an intrusion on her sister's social life, which, according to Harry, was non-existent. "Are you sure you want me to come back?"

"Of course I want you to come back," Kim responded quickly. "I'd like for the two of us to spend some more time together before you leave."

"I don't want to intrude into your schedule."

"Don't be silly. It isn't that I don't want to see you." There was a pleading in Kim's eyes. "It's just that…it's that I have other things to take care of this morning."

Obviously, Susan thought.

She had parked her car off to the side of the driveway. When she walked away from the house, she cut across the lawn instead of following the flagstone pathway. As she strode across the long grass, out of the corner of her eye, she caught sight of the trunk portion of a slate blue car protruding from behind the house. It had been a man in a blue car who had signaled to turn into the driveway the first day she had gone out to see Kim. Susan remembered the mirrored glasses. The bearded face.

Was Kyle Markum Kim's overnight guest? The possibility of her sister having an affair with Gil Markum's son left a strange taste in her mouth. Kim had vowed she would get even with Gil for what had happened to her husband. No mention had been made of Kyle, but surely he would benefit from the family's business profits which, according to Kim, was the reason the car had been tested prematurely. As a member of the Markum family, and the inventor of the failed automotive part, he was just as responsible for Brad's death as Gil was, wasn't he? Possibly more so.

The sun peeked in and out from behind the clouds as Susan drove back to town, but already the heat of the day was beginning to lie over the area like melting cheese.

The answering machine was blinking when Susan walked in the door of Harry's house. She pressed 'Play' and heard his voice. 'Thought I'd check to see if you've changed your mind about going out to Kim's."

"I'm going out there later this afternoon," Susan told him minutes later when she called him at the newspaper office.

"How late this afternoon?" Harry wanted to know.

"Around four. Why?"

"I'm interviewin' some people at the Country Club for a feature story for the Trib. Why don't you come out and we'll talk, maybe have a drink or some lunch. With me workin' all the time, we haven't been able to spend much time together."

"Do they let non-members on the grounds?" Susan asked.

"If they don't, I'll say nasty things about them in my article."

Susan laughed. "I'll see you later." She needed to talk to Harry, to tell him that she would be leaving for California soon. She couldn't put Mark off much longer if there was to be a chance of reconciliation between them.

"Do you think your sister noticed anything?" the man with Kim asked as he pushed his arm into the sleeve of his suitcoat.

Kim shrugged. "I don't know, but I'll give her a call and soothe her ruffled feathers. She's becoming a little put out with me."

Pulling Kim into his arms, he kissed her hungrily.

"Don't you think you'd better go to work?" she said when he released her.

He grinned down at her. "I was thinking of calling in sick so I could stay a little longer."

Kim laughed. "Aren't you afraid you'll lose your job if you don't show up for work once in a while?" They had spent the last two nights and part of yesterday together. They had made love and made plans and made love again. Now if only she could get rid of the Weasel.

Kim moaned softly as the man holding her brushed his lips across her cheek. Then he sought her mouth and covered it with his own once again.

"Just think," he murmured into her ear. "Soon we won't have to sneak around like this." He buried his face in the softness of her long pale hair. "We'll be far away. We'll have a new life, a life together."

Drawing back, Kim peered into his eyes. "Are you sure that's what you want?"

"Do you need to ask?" he asked, his voice husky with emotion.

The shrill ringing of the telephone made them leap apart, as if a knife had sliced down between them. Kim stiffened, her heart thudding in her rib cage. If that was who she was afraid it was....

"I'll leave you to answer your phone," her lover said. "See you later."

After the door closed behind him, Kim let the phone ring a half dozen more times before she lifted the receiver. When the voice spoke in her ear, she recognized it immediately. She saw The Weasel's shifty eyes, his long thin face.

"Got any more info on that security system yet?" he asked.

"I can't find out anything worthwhile."

"Try harder."

"I'll arouse suspicion if I ask too many questions. Why do you need so much information about the system? I thought you knew what you were doing."

"So I exaggerated a little. I need to know as much as I can about it so I can deactivate the sensors."

"If you're caught you'll be arrested."

"If I'm caught we'll <u>both</u> be arrested, Sweetheart, so you'd better come up with something to make sure that doesn't happen."

"You won't be able to pull this thing off," Kim said again, seeing a way out. "You've been feeding me a bunch of bullshit. Let's forget the whole thing."

"No way. If I can get in and out without anyone knowing it, I may be able to tap that tree again, the next time Junior comes up with another brilliant idea. You'd better get me some code numbers, some info on those sensors or else...."

"Or else what?" Kim challenged.

"Or else I'll make an anonymous phone call and let your little playmate in on what's been goin' on—the real reason you've been dishin' out the goodies to him."

Kim's hand was clammy as she gripped the receiver. "You wouldn't."

"I would. I don't like to be crossed. How do you think I got this scar on my face? I got in a fight with a guy who tried to renege on a deal we'd made. You don't wanna hear what happened to him."

A likely story, Kim thought. The Weasel liked to brag about how macho he was. "I'll go to my friend and tell him everything," she vowed in desperation. "He loves me. He'll forgive me."

There was a pause on the other end of the line. Kim could almost hear the cogs churning in The Weasel's wily mind.

"Maybe. But Old Man Markum won't be so understandin' or forgivin'."

"You're in this as deep as I am. You'll be cutting your own throat."

"I'll make a deal with him. In exchange for my neck and a chunk of green, I'll give him the name of the person who's been tryin' to put him out business. He'll go for it. He's a vindictive man. It makes me queasy just thinkin' about what he'll do to you."

She couldn't allow the Weasel to blackmail her. She had to try once more to get him to back off. "I can't find out anything important. Get real. He's not going to discuss the security system with me or anyone else."

"You'd better give it another try. You're a talented girl. Surely you know how to loosen up a guy. Give him an extra roll between the sheets," the Weasel urged. "Maybe we'd better have a little chat. I'm comin' out."

"It won't do you any good."

"Look, Sweetheart. I don't like to be double-crossed."

Kim's mouth tightened. "And I don't like to be pushed."

If he showed up, she would be ready for him. Never fully trusting him, she had prepared for something like this. She had provided herself with a way out, and she would use it if she had to. Admittedly, she had been having second thoughts about doing something so drastic, but he was giving her little choice.

Chapter 16

The Country Club's manicured grounds stretched from the clubhouse across the rolling acres with its carefully spaced hazards and sand traps to the white sands along Lake Sally's shore. Golfers clad in colorful sports attire drove carts or walked about the greens with bags of clubs draped over their shoulders. A quick glance at her watch told Susan it was almost three o'clock. She had timed her arrival at the club so she wouldn't get there until her uncle had completed his interviews.

As she entered the lounge, she spotted Harry sitting at a corner table. He wasn't alone. Susan recognized the burly shoulders and thatch of snowy white hair immediately. Remembering the intimacy they had shared, she wondered, once again, if Gil were truly interested in her or if she were merely the new girl in town. Someone to be checked out. Or was she being too distrustful? Was everyone misjudging him, making him out to be an uncaring monster when he didn't deserve the title? From what little she had seen of him, admittedly he was intimidating, and, no doubt, accustomed to getting what he wanted. But that was no crime. And she had a sister like that.

Susan hesitated, unsure if she should interrupt the two men. Her uncle motioned to her, and when she reached his table, both men rose. Gil's thick white hair appeared to be damp, as if he had stepped out of the shower a short time ago. As she stood next to him, the fragrance of his expensive cologne filled her nostrils. It was the same cologne he had been wearing the night before. Her blood warmed at the memory of his touch.

His eyes widened in surprise at the sight of her. "Susan, how nice to see you again."

Remembering Harry's disapproval of Gil, Susan gave him a small smile. "It's nice to see you, too."

"What are you doing here?" he asked. "Is Harry interviewing you, too?"

"Susan is my niece. I invited her to join me for lunch after the interview," Harry said, motioning for Susan to sit down.

Gil's eyes widened in surprise. "Your niece! You mentioned an uncle, Susan, and you two were together the first time we met, but I didn't realize.... How dense of me."

"My wife and I raised Susan's sister, Kim Hastings, after their mother died," Harry added.

There was a tightening of the muscles along Gil's strong jaw, a sharpening in his steely blue eyes as he eased his large frame back onto his chair. "You didn't tell me Kim Hastings was your sister." It was more of an accusation than a statement.

"I didn't think of it. I didn't know it mattered." But she had been afraid it might, and that was why she hadn't said anything.

Harry was staring at her questioningly, clearly puzzled by the familiarity between her and Gil. Harry opened his mouth as if to say something and then, apparently decided against it.

With an effort, Gil composed himself and flashed Susan a quick smile. "It doesn't matter."

The expression on his face told her it mattered a great deal. His eyes had darkened and filled with shadows, making them opaque, shutting off whatever he was thinking. She wondered why he was suddenly so distant. Although he was doing his best to conceal it, she sensed he was badly shaken.

Was he aware Kim held him responsible for Brad's death? Although it should be obvious to Gil that Harry didn't like him, it shouldn't matter to him that Harry was her uncle. Gil should be accustomed to people who disliked him for one reason or another. Perhaps envious of his achievements, they told themselves his accomplishments had been gained by illegal means, whether or not it was true.

"Have you been staying at your sister's place while you're in town?" Gil asked.

"Part of the time," Susan acknowledged.

"No wonder I've had the feeling I should know you." Gil spoke with constrained lightness. "You look like your sister."

"So you know Kim?" Susan ventured cautiously.

"Not personally." His tanned face was impassive, like a mask carved from mahogany. "But I've met her."

There was a fluttering in the pit of Susan's stomach. Had Kim confronted him and accused him of killing Brad?

Susan saw the tautness of Gil's jaw muscles, the furrowing of his forehead between his dark, bushy brows. As the heavy silence persisted, Susan felt as though they were in a huge, dark void instead of the sunny, many-windowed lounge.

"I'm sorry, Susan." Harry's voice filled the silence that had enveloped them like a shroud. "I'd hoped to finish with this interview by the time you arrived, but Gil was late gettin' here."

"I'll leave the two of you alone until you're through." Susan made a motion to rise. Gil's eyes, as he studied her, were making her uncomfortable.

"That's okay," Harry told her. "I'm sure Gil doesn't mind. We'll be finished in a few minutes. No article about the Country Club would be complete without interviewin' its most prominent member."

Harry's eyes flickered to the scratches on Gil's arm, drawing Susan's attention to them. "Looks like the business that held you up had to do with a tom cat."

Glancing down at his arm, Gil laughed lightly. "Oh, these. I was walking over the grounds behind my house this morning, and got into an argument with some bushes."

As the two men continued their conversation, with Harry taking notes, Susan sensed Gil's uneasiness. He was, she conjectured wryly, eager to get the interview over with and leave.

As he spoke quietly, making concise, informative statements, Susan sensed the aura of power about him. She knew, without hesitation, that when he wanted to impose his will, he influenced subordinates and business associates alike by lapsing into the same quiet manner of speech.

Then the interview was over and Gil stood up, towering over her as she sat at the table.

"See you around." He gave her a cool smile, then turned to Harry. "It's been a pleasure talking with you. I'm looking forward to reading your article."

He walked away, leaving Susan staring after him in bewilderment, her heart plunging. "See you around," he'd said, as if she were merely an acquaintance instead of the woman he had held in his arms and wanted to make love to the previous afternoon. He was acting as if the intimacy they had spent together hadn't transpired. Was she making too much of it? she wondered, while he, quite possibly, was considering it as insignificant, just a few hours with a willing conquest.

Harry reached out and squeezed Susan's hand clumsily. "I think it's time for a drink." He gestured for the waitress. When she reached the table, he ordered two double martinis. "I think the lady needs a little somethin' extra."

When the drinks arrived, Susan took a long swallow of the drink he had ordered for her, choked as the liquor burned a fiery trail down her throat.

"What was that all about?" Harry's eyes were filled with an expression of bewilderment behind his wire-rimmed glasses.

"What was what all about?" Susan asked, pretending not to know what he was talking out.

"That 'nice to see you again' stuff. That 'why are you doing this to me' look."

"It doesn't matter...."

Harry studied her for a long moment. "Yeah, I can tell."

"What have you got against Gil?" Susan asked. "What's he done to you?"

Harry lifted his thin, bony shoulders in a shrug. "You know how it is when you meet someone and you don't like the guy at the git go, but you don't have a legitimate reason. That's the way I feel about Gil Markum. However, everyone doesn't share my feelings. He's on the 'Most Eligible Bachelor' list of every female in the area. His is the name people drop when they want to impress someone."

Glancing down at her watch, Susan saw that it was four o'clock, the time she was supposed to be at Kim's place. *Let her wonder if I'm coming,* Susan thought in defiance. *It'll do her good.*

Harry's gaze was fixed on Susan's face. "I know it's none of my business, but what's goin' on between you and Gil Markum?"

"Nothing's going on." If Gil's actions were any indication, Susan sensed that the statement might well be true.

Chapter 17

As she swung the corner into Kim's driveway, Susan wondered if this trip was another dry run. If it turned out to be, Kim would have to come to her the next time. Then Susan's attention was caught by the sight of a dark form sprawled on the grass along the walkway.

My God! Something had happened to Kim!

When she drew closer, Susan saw that it wasn't her sister's body but that of a man. He was lying on his stomach, his arms outstretched. Her blood chilled; the core of her soul went dead. Kim had shot someone, as she had said she could and would do if she had to! Cold currents slithered up and down Susan's spine.

She braked her car to a halt and slowly, carefully, climbed out. The man was dead, she sensed as she forced herself to move closer to him.

Not just motionless, just lifeless, but horribly, shockingly torn and ugly, his body shattered. Blood stained the back of his shirt. It was in his hair, streaking the dark fibrous mass, matting it in places. Drawn by the sweet scent of the blood, a green-bodied fly buzzed around his head. By the brightness of the blood, Susan knew he hadn't been dead long. Of average build, he was wearing faded jeans and a short-sleeved shirt that had seen better days.

It appeared as if he had been shot in the back while leaving—or running away from the house. His fingers were spread claw-like as he lay outstretched on the grass. There were marks in the ground alongside the walk, as if he had been clutching at the grass, attempting to hold on to life by its long, thin blades.

Hoping that, somehow, it wasn't true, that she was experiencing a bad dream, Susan halted. Standing a few feet from him, she forced herself to look down. Her face lurched, and for a moment, she thought she was going to be sick.

The man's face was turned to the side. She saw a large, hooked nose, a thin, bony face. An old scar extended across his cheek and into his bloodied hairline. There was blood on the side of his face, too, and in the creases of his scrawny neck.

Horror choking her, Susan felt bile rising in her throat once again. Quickly, she stepped over to a tree. Clutching it, she threw up, continued to retch after her stomach was emptied, until her throat was raw and her chest ached. She shivered at the cold sweat that prickled the skin under her arms and on her back.

The wind whispered eerily in the pine boughs around her.

A deep disquiet swept through her. Was her sister dead inside the house? Someone had tried to break in before, had beaten and tried to rape her. Had it happened again, or was this something far worse?

Or had Kim committed this heinous crime?

"Kim?" Susan's voice was cracked and tremulous with fear as her gaze turned toward the house. In the surrounding silence, her voice sounded hollow in her ears. Fear gripping her, Susan wondered if Kim was in the house, another bloodied victim of a crazed killer.

"Kim?" Susan's voice rose shrilly.

Legs trembling like pillars of jello, she stumbled toward the house. When she reached the steps, she saw that the door was partially open. Cautiously, she pushed it with her foot, taking care not to touch the knob or the door frame, to obliterate any fingerprints left there.

Throat dry and tasting of bile, she called out Kim's name again. Heart pounding, she glanced about the room, fearful that at any moment, her gaze would fall upon the inert and bloodied form of her sister.

Nothing seemed out of place. On the kitchen table was the evidence of lunch—a half-eaten sandwich, three quarters of a cup of cold coffee.

Food on the table; a partially opened door—

Susan hurried toward the bedroom. Hesitating in the doorway, she croaked harshly, "Kim?"

She heard no sound anywhere in the house except the wild, pained beating of her heart. She sagged against the door frame, nausea rising in her throat once again. *Dear God. Please, my sister didn't do this.*

But where was she? If this man had tried to harm her and she had shot him in self-defense, why had she run away? Had she panicked? Or hadn't she been alone? Had her overnight guest been with her when this had occurred? Could it be that this was the man who had spent the night with her?

The dead man appeared to be in his late forties or early fifties. Susan had difficulty envisioning this scar-faced creature as her sister's paramour. Or had the idea of Kim having a lover been the product of her imagination? Could her sister's visitor have been a friend or neighbor who had stopped by?

Her breath lodged in her throat, Susan stepped into the bedroom.

"Kim?" Her voice dashed against the walls, and bounce back toward her.

The faint fragrance of perfume still hovered in the air. Susan took a deep breath, as if by inhaling, she could draw Kim closer. She looked about, praying, wishing her sister to materialize out of the emptiness. Where was she, for God's sake? Had she disappeared of her own volition? The possibility that she had been killed or forcibly abducted balanced on the edge of Susan's mind.

Slowly, cautiously, she advanced into the center of the room. She felt that if she turned around, Kim would be behind her, tossing her long pale hair off her shoulders and telling her, in an annoyed tone of voice, to stop worrying. That she could take care of herself. *Please, God. Make it be true!*

Numbly, as if she were in a trance, Susan picked up a framed snapshot from atop the dresser and stared at it. The picture was of Kim and Brad in a sailboat. They were waving and smiling. The glass felt cool and smooth to Susan's touch. How happy Kim had been then. How different she appeared now. Closing her eyes, Susan saw, again, the haunted look in her sister's dark eyes, the grim set of her lips. A rush of love and compassion swept over her. *Oh, Kim, what's happened to you? I can't believe you did this terrible thing!*

Nothing's happened to Kim, Susan told herself, repeating the words like a charm. Bad things didn't happened to her sister. Kim was the one who'd had the perfect marriage. The one who did as she pleased, who'd always gotten everything she wanted.

It was more of a sudden prickly feeling on the surface of her skin rather than any sound she heard that made Susan realize with an undefinable shock, that she was no longer alone. She spun around, her mouth agape and her hand on her throat. "Kim?"

When Susan recognized the tall, uniformed figure of Reid Elison, she released a ragged sigh—of disappointment or relief, she wasn't sure which.

"I...I was looking for Kim," she stammered. "I just got here a few minutes ago." She gestured helplessly. "I found that man outside...."

"Your sister isn't here?" Reid glanced about the bedroom. When Susan shook her head, he asked, "What about her car? Is that gone, too?"

"I...I don't know. I didn't check...." Susan followed behind Reid as he went into the kitchen. He opened the door that led into the garage, then turned around.

"The car's not here."

Gone was the saddened and bereft man who had revealed the pain he felt at the loss of his wife. In its place was a stern-faced lawman once again. The brief period of camaraderie he and Susan shared over dinner seemed to have occurred in another time.

She spoke numbly, as if her tongue were partially anesthetized. "Kim asked me to come out this afternoon. She said we would go out to dinner...." Susan groped out for something to hold onto.

Reid took hold of her arm. "Are you okay?"

"Yes...I don't know...Oh, God!" She buried her face in her hands. "Where is she? What's happened to her?"

Reid placed his hand on Susan's arm, but no bodily warmth could ameliorate the coldness that gripped her. Previously, whenever something had gone amiss, she had closed her mind to the pain and had tried to erase it from her thoughts. She had told herself it would pass. But she was aware that some things couldn't be wished away. This was one of them.

Holding onto her arm, Reid led her outside.

The thought that Kim had bought a gun for protection weighed on Susan's mind. Her sister had boasted of her ability to use it, had stressed that she wouldn't hesitate to do so. Susan gave the dead man a quick darting look. Had she used it on him? "How...how did you find out about him?"

"Some guy who had come out to repair the television set called us," Reid explained. He peered down at the lifeless form lying on the grass. "Do you know him?"

Susan shook her head from side to side in denial. "Kim didn't do this. My sister couldn't have done such a terrible thing." The man had been shot in the back of the head. Kim couldn't have murdered another human being in cold blood. Not Kim, no matter how much she had changed.

"Let's see who we have." Squatting on his haunches, Reid began to search the dead man's pockets. He removed some loose change, a pack of USA Golds and a Zippo lighter.

There was no wallet, Susan noted in spite of her overwrought condition. Everyone carries a wallet, don't they? she thought through the fog in her mind. Had it been removed to make it more difficult to identify him?

Reid stood up, carefully checking the contents from the dead man's pockets. Then, opening a notebook, he made a quick sketch of the yard, noting the position of the front steps and the walkway in relation to the body sprawled on the grass. When he had finished, he handed his tape measure to another deputy who was standing nearby. The deputy painstakingly measured the distances between the various objects in the yard, calling out figures Reid entered into his sketch. After they had finished, a medical examiner knelt down by the dead man.

The medic lifted one of the dead man's arms. "He's as lifeless as a rock."

"With his brains spilling out on the lawn, I'd say that's a likely condition," the deputy said.

"Don't move him until we've gotten some pictures," Reid instructed.

"From the condition of his body, he's been dead a couple of hours or so," the medical examiner said. "When I get him in the morgue and do an examination, I'll be able to tell you more."

The scene was like a slow-motion ballet as Susan watched each man move to his appointed task.

"Okay, guys, load him up," Reid directed. "Johnson, you can cordon off the area now."

Reid turned his attention to Susan. "Do you know where your sister could have gone?"

Susan shook her head. "Maybe she wasn't home…hasn't been home all afternoon. Maybe she doesn't know about this…."

By the expression in Reid's eyes, Susan could see that he was aware she was grasping at straws.

"Surely you don't believe Kim did this!" Susan burst out. "Oh, God! What's happened to her?"

Reid took hold of Susan's arm again, steadied her. "We'll find her." He spoke with confidence, but Susan wasn't so certain.

She glanced around the yard. How had the dead man gotten out here? Except for her own car and the vehicles belonging to Reid and the medical team, there was no sign of another vehicle. Had the dead man walked, possibly from a lake home nearby? Or had there been two of them, and the other one had fled when his partner was shot?

The questions clutched at her. If this had been another break-in attempt and Kim had been defending herself, why had she run away? No one would blame her for protecting herself.

Susan couldn't put the memory of the morning out of her mind. She suspected that Kyle Markum had been her sister's visitor. Had he played a part in this heinous deed? Had he and Kim fled together, or had Kyle left before it had occurred? It was entirely possible that he had been the last person to see Kim. Perhaps they had gone off somewhere *before* the man had been killed. If that had happened, why and who had killed the dead man?

Around and around the thoughts and suppositions whirled in Susan's brain.

It was all too confusing. Too overwhelming. Her head was pounding from the innumerable questions she sought to have answered. In desperation, she placed her hands over her ears and closed her eyes tightly in an effort to stop the questions from spinning in her head.

"I'll drive you back to Harry's place," Reid offered.

Susan opened her eyes and looked at him. He didn't have time to act as her baby sitter. He had a murder on his hands. Perhaps two murders.

No! No! She mustn't think that way! Kim hadn't been murdered. She wasn't dead. Not Kim. There had to be a logical explanation for her disappearance. Maybe she wasn't aware of what had happened at her home. Maybe she would reappear at any moment, and be just as bewildered and horrified as everyone else. Maybe she….

Chapter 18

Susan was too shaken to protest Reid's offer to drive her car back to Harry's place for her. The deputy, whom Reid had referred to as 'Johnson' brought the patrol car back to town.

When the three of them reached the house, Reid came inside and called the newspaper office to inform Harry about what had happened. When he hung up, Reid said, "Harry's left for the day. Is there someone I can call to come and stay with you?"

"Don't worry about me," Susan said quickly. "I'll be okay. Just find out what's happened to my sister."

"I've never been involved in a homicide," Deputy Johnson said as Reid replaced him behind the steering wheel of the patrol car. "Do you know who the dead man is? I've never seen him before."

Reid turned on the ignition. "Don't know him." The car's engine leapt to life. Shifting into 'Drive', he checked the traffic before pulling into the street.

Deputy Johnson turned to him with a puzzled expression on his face. "What do you think's going on out there?"

"I wish to hell I knew," Reid growled. The more he thought about the case, the angrier he became. And the more inadequate he felt.

Most crimes, at least violent crimes, involved family members or lovers. But that didn't appear to be the case here. So what *was* going on? He'd had some pretty weird cases when he was on the Phoenix police force and had solved most of them. Why hadn't he been able to figure out what was going on at Kim Hastings' place before someone had been murdered?"

"Looks like the Hastings woman killed the guy and split," Deputy Johnson concluded.

"Looks that way."

"Not very bright to shoot someone on your doorstep. The police are bound to think you killed him."

"People panic when they realize they've done something wrong," Reid pointed out. "The guy was small but he was dead weight. I don't think she could have put him in her car and dumped him in a road ditch."

Susan watched out the window as the deputies drove away, then squeezed her eyes shut. What now? Had Harry found out what had happened and taken a different road out to Kim's place? No, more likely he had stopped for a beer after work, and was unaware of what had taken place.

Susan's thoughts went to Kyle Markum. She hadn't told Reid about him. She wasn't entirely sure Kyle had been Kim's overnight guest. She had to make certain, to talk to him, and find out if he knew about the dead man. Fingers trembling, she paged through the phone book until she found Markum Manufacturing.

"If you'll hold, I'll see if Mr. Markum is in," a cool, efficient voice said when Susan asked for Kyle.

Several minutes later, he was on the line.

"I'd like to talk to you," Susan told him. "It's about Kim."

"Who is this?" Kyle's voice was cautious.

"This is Kim's sister, Susan Edwards. I met you in front of Miller's Cafe several days ago, remember?"

"Oh, yes," Kyle acknowledged. Then he was silent. Waiting.

"Were you at Kim's place this morning when I was out there?" Susan asked.

The only response was a buzzing noise on the line as she held the phone against her ear.

"Do you know where my sister is?" she implored, her voice breaking.

"What are you talking about?" Kyle demanded. "She's at home, isn't she?"

"No, she's not there. Something's happened. I need to talk to you. Could we meet somewhere?"

"Has something happened to Kim?" There was anxiety in Kyle's voice.

Without having to be told, Susan was certain that it had been Kyle's suit coat that was draped over the chair at Kim's place. "I...we can't discuss this on the phone. How about Miller's Cafe in a half hour?"

Twenty minutes later, Susan found Kyle sitting in a corner booth, a cup of coffee in front of him. The small cafe was empty except for a middle-aged waitress and two elderly couples seated at tables across the room. Kyle stood up as Susan approached, then sat down again as she slid onto the worn vinyl seat across from him. The expression on his face was anxious but wary.

"So help me if you're playing some sort of game," he warned.

"I don't play games with murder."

His bearded jaw gaped. "Murder! My God! You're not telling me that Kim was...."

"I don't know what's happened to her." Slowly, in a voice heavy with dread, Susan told him of her grisly discovery.

Kyle's face was ashen, his eyes wide with horror. "Someone tried to break in again!"

"All I know is that a man is dead and Kim is gone. What time did you leave her place?"

"A little before one o'clock."

If he were telling the truth, in Susan's judgment, it was unlikely he was the one who had killed the man at Kim's place. If the medical examiner were correct, the man hadn't been dead that long. Yet, there wasn't all that much difference in the time. Without the benefit of an autopsy, the medical examiner could have been off an hour or so. Leaning forward, Susan peered into Kyle's face. "What's been going on between you and my sister?"

"That's none of your business."

"I don't care about your love life. I care about my sister. Do you have any idea where she could have gone?"

Kyle shook his head. "She had to have gone on an errand or something before you got there."

"I keep telling myself that," Susan told him. "Are you sure you left Kim's place before one?"

Kyle nodded. "I went home, changed clothes, and checked in the plant at one thirty."

"What excuse did you give your wife for spending the night away from home?"

"Marisa wasn't there. She went to visit her parents. Her father hasn't been well lately. She was due home early this afternoon." He glanced down at his watch. "She's probably there now."

"Do you know where Kim might go if she didn't want to be found?"

Kyle's knuckles were white, his shoulders hunched in despair as he clutched his coffee cup. He shook his head from side to side. "I have no idea."

"Surely you must know of some place, of someone she could go to." Susan could not keep the desperation out of her voice.

Savagely, Kyle shoved his fingers through his tawny hair. "I don't know! I can't think! Surely you don't believe Kim killed that man!"

"My heart tells me she didn't." Her head told her she didn't know her sister at all.

The waitress halted beside the booth, and Susan ordered a cup of black coffee. "Did Kim mention she was going anyplace after you left her?" Susan probed after the coffee was served.

"She said that you and she were going out for dinner this evening."

Susan described the dead man. "Do you know anyone who fits that description?

Again, Kyle shook his head. "Did you tell Reid Elison that you saw me at Kim's?"

Susan told him that she hadn't.

"You can't tell him."

"My sister is missing. She may be dead and you're concerned about your reputation?" Susan raged, her eyes blazing.

Shaking his head, Kyle's gaze bore into hers. "That's not what I'm worried about. I'm as concerned about Kim as you are. I love her. And yes, I spent the night with her. But it's imperative that our relationship be kept quiet for a little longer. I'm an industrial engineer. I've been working on a new project. The whole thing will blow up if it gets out about us before this project is finished."

Susan's fingers gripped the handle of her coffee cup. "Then help me find her."

"I'll tear the place apart if I have to." Kyle's tone was adamant. Determined. "But no one must know I'm the one doing it."

"Because of your name and your job?" Susan tried to hold back the thoughts churning inside her head. They were too distasteful to consider. "What part does Marisa play in all of this? Does she know about you and Kim?"

"I don't think so. At least, she hasn't confronted me about it. Marisa forced me into a marriage I didn't want, and she won't let go." Kyle's voice was bitter. "My father is against my divorcing her, too."

Kyle took a swallow of coffee, then set the cup down. "I need time to finish the new project I'm working on. I don't want anything to go wrong this time. A year ago, we tested a new concept I'd developed. We were in a hurry to get it on the market before our competitors did.

The test car exploded and the driver was killed. That driver was Brad Hastings."

"And out of guilt, you felt you had to comfort his wife?" Susan ventured in an accusatory tone.

"I knew Kim was shattered by Brad's death. I felt sorry for her. And yes, guilty, too, for letting my father talk me into permitting something to be tested before it had been perfected. I went to see Kim to express my condolences, and to see if I could help her in any way. We fell in love."

Kyle might be in love, Susan thought as she studied him. But up until this morning, Kim hadn't acted like a woman in love. She had been a vengeful woman, a woman determined to avenge the death of the husband she had adored. "How does Kim feel about you being married?"

"She's willing to go along with me until later, even if it's risky. If our relationship were to become known at this time, it might mean the loss of millions of dollars worth of contracts for Markum Manufacturing."

Susan frowned. "I don't understand."

"If Marisa's father finds out I'm involved with another woman, he'll have our contracts canceled. He has a lot of clout in high places. He could put Markum Manufacturing out of business."

Susan glared across the table at Kyle. "So it's business first."

His cheeks reddened slightly. "I owe my father that much."

Placing her hands in her lap, Susan clasped them tightly together. Just days ago she had been thinking how dull and sterile her life had become since her divorce. Now she felt as if she had been thrust into a hurricane. No...more aptly, what she was experiencing was a nightmare from which there seemed to be no escape.

"This thing could get messy if the city presses got hold of it," Kyle pointed out. "Can't you see the headlines? 'MISSING WOMAN INVOLVED IN LOVE TRIANGLE'. Small towns thrive on gossip, rumors, and speculation." He glanced at the couple sitting across the room from them. Susan had noticed the two of them glancing at her and Kyle from time to time, whispering covertly.

"I'll bet they're wondering what the two of us are doing together," Kyle said with disdain. "They can't wait to tell everyone about it."

"I couldn't care less what they're thinking," Susan said tersely. "All I want is to know where my sister is."

"So do I," Kyle defended. "It's not only the company I'm worried about. Think what something like that would do to Kim. She's been through enough."

Susan pondered his words for a moment, then silently agreed with them. His reasoning sounded plausible, his concerns genuine. Kim wasn't the only one who would be caught up in the scandal. Harry lived here, too. Kim could move away and begin a new life if she chose to, but Harry's roots were entrenched in this small town where he had lived all his life, and his parents before him.

"When the project is perfected and on the market, I'm divorcing Marisa, no matter what she or my father say. Kim and I are going away together." Kyle shoved his cup back, away from him. "Are you sure *you* don't know where she could have gone?"

"If I did, I wouldn't have called you."

Kyle drew in a ragged breath, then released it. "I wish I could help you. I'm as concerned about her as you are. I promise I'll do everything I can to find Kim. I'm certain she wasn't home when that man was killed. I know she isn't responsible for what happened to him."

"I hope not," a grave-faced Susan said as she stood up. She had to find Harry and tell him what had happened. She wondered if he were home from work yet.

Kyle remained seated at the table, as if he were uncertain what to do.

After paying for her coffee and as she shoved open the door that led out of the restaurant, Susan had to step back abruptly to avoid colliding with Marisa Markum. The ebony-haired woman was dressed in white slacks that fit her slender, leggy figure to perfection, and a striped red and white top that enhanced her bronze skin. Her long, dark hair swayed slightly as she jerked back.

"I noticed Kyle's car parked outside. I saw you and him through the window." Marisa's green eyes were icy. "What's my husband got that you and your bitch of a sister find so irresistible?"

"I had to talk to him," Susan explained, ignoring Marisa's biting comment. "So you're back. How's your father?"

Brows arching, Marisa's lips curled in a mirthless smile. "Don't tell me you and Kyle were discussing my father's health."

"He mentioned your father wasn't well. I want to talk to you."

Marisa's slender frame stiffened. "About what?"

"To start with, I'd like to know what you meant the other day when you said the attempted break-in at my sister's place made a good story."

"It was meant the way it sounded." Marisa made a move to push past Susan, but Susan reached out and placed her hand firmly on Marisa's tanned arm.

"Let's talk about that."

Adjusting the strap on the white handbag draped over her shoulder, Marisa measured Susan with icy disdain. "I don't have time." She jerked her arm out of Susan's grasp.

"You'd better make time—unless you'd like to come with me to the police station."

Marisa's eyes remained defiant for a moment. Then they wavered.

"My car's in the parking lot," Susan told her.

"Before we begin, I'd like to set you straight on a few things," Marisa said minutes later as she slid into the Skyhawk. Her cold eyes slashed through Susan like a razor. "I despise your little sister. But then most wives hate the woman their husband's crawling into the sack with, don't they?"

"If you knew about it, why didn't you try to stop it?" Susan challenged.

"It's more complicated than that. You wouldn't understand."

"Try me."

All the fight seemed to seep out of Marisa. "I've been crazy about Kyle since I was a kid. But he didn't see me until I was eighteen. We started dating. I was *in* love. He wanted to *make* love. End results—if you get a senator's daughter pregnant and she won't have an abortion, you marry her whether you want to or not. Especially if her daddy and your daddy say so." Marisa's brittle laughter was laden with cynicism.

"Kyle agreed to go through with the rituals, but he lives his life and I try to live mine." Marisa shrugged her shoulders. "What else can I do? Besides, I've had the childish notion that some day Kyle would fall in love with me. It might have happened if your sister hadn't come into the picture." Bitterness burned in her voice like acid into flesh.

Susan was silent, waiting for Marisa to go on.

"Kyle hates me because he thinks I trapped him. And I don't even have his child. I miscarried." Marisa paused, pain etched on her face. "When I found out about Kyle and Kim, I went to Gil, hoping he would put an end to the affair. All he said was that I should hang in there. That it would burn itself out. He warned me that if I got pushy with Kyle, he might walk out on the new project he's working on."

"I think Gil was afraid that if he were to interfere in Kyle's personal life too much, Kyle would walk out on me. Not that Gil cares about me. It's what my daddy can do for him that concerns Gil."

Susan flinched at Marisa's derogatory remarks about the man who's apparent rejection, after he learned she was Kim's sister, still weighed heavily on her mind. Was Gil that heartless or was Marisa exaggerating? Susan felt empathy for the lovely girl-woman who had just bared her soul. "This still doesn't explain what you meant about the break-in attempt being a good story."

"I'm coming to that," Marisa said. "But first, I want you to know that I think your sister is up to something besides fooling around with my husband. Something awfully weird...."

In view of what had happened an hour or so ago, Susan was afraid to hear Marisa's answer. Yet she had to know. It might unlock some doors, and uncover some truths. Possibly, it would provide information about Kim's whereabouts. "Why do you think Kim is up to something?"

"After I found out that she and Kyle were sleeping together, I called your sister's place several times intending to tell her what I thought of her. But I chickened out when I heard her voice. Then I drove out to her place. I don't know what I intended to do. Demand. Beg. Tear out her hair..." Marisa's voice cracked, and she took a ragged breath.

"Kim didn't answer the doorbell. I was about to leave when a huge dog darted out of the woods nearby and started barking at me. Kim was on the beach. When she heard him, she came toward the house. I could see her coming, but she couldn't see me. The shrubbery alongside the house blocked her view of the front door."

"Anyway, she ran up the stones steps at the end of the lawn. She must have caught her toe. She stumbled, fell forward on the steps, and struck her head. When she got to her feet, she was bleeding badly from a cut on her forehead. I couldn't bring myself to confront her with blood streaming down her face, but I wasn't about to play nursemaid either. I ran back to my car and took off. Apparently, she didn't know I was there."

Marisa's explanation whirled in Susan's head, sending her thoughts spinning off in all directions, yet answering nothing. Impatiently, she waited for Marisa to go on.

The dark-haired woman's piercing green eyes met Susan's with condemnation. "Then the story came out in the newspaper that your sister had caught someone trying to break into her place, that he had man-handled her, tried to rape her. Her clothing was torn—so she said—and she received a gash on her forehead."

Marisa halted, obviously waiting for her words to have an effect.

Susan frowned, still unable to grasp the meaning of the dark-haired woman's statement. "I don't understand...."

"The story was a hoax. There was no burglar, no attempted break-in. No assault."

"How do you know?" Susan asked. She was uncertain if Marisa was telling the truth, or if she was the one who was perpetrating a hoax. "Why should Kim make up a story like that? The break-in could have occurred after you left."

"The newspaper stated that Kim had reported the break-in attempt at two thirty, which was the exact time I was there. I know, because I checked my watch while I was waiting for her to answer the doorbell. The story your sister gave the authorities was a pack of lies. She received the cut on her forehead when she fell on the steps while I was there. She must have torn her own clothing to back up her story."

Susan tried to comprehend everything Marisa had told her, tried to put it into perspective. Emerging was a portrait of her sister she didn't like. Ungrateful daughter. Embittered avenger. Adulteress. Liar. Susan knew few people were what others expected them to be, but she accepted that. Conceivably, Kim was depressed and unhappy, but she wasn't all those other things that Marisa made her out to be.

Where are you, Kim? Susan anguished. *Why aren't you here defending yourself?*

Susan squeezed her eyes shut to stop the fears that churned inside her. How much of what Marisa said was true? Was she simply being spiteful by casting incredulity on Kim? How much of her statement were the words of a woman who felt cheated and still hoped to regain the love of the man she was married to?

Marisa's overt hostility toward her and the accusations against Kim stirred Susan's anger. "If you thought Kim's story was a hoax, why didn't you tell the authorities?"

"Are you kidding? How would I have explained my knowing that?" Marisa's scornful attitude was resurfacing. "Gil would have killed me if he'd known I went out to Kim's place after he told me to let it alone. Just like he would kill me now if he knew I told you all of this."

"I went out to Kim's place this afternoon," Susan told Marisa. "She wasn't there, but I found a dead man on her doorstep."

"A dead man!" Marisa's face was ashen. "Is that...is that why you were talking to Kyle? Surely you don't think he had anything to do with that!"

"At this point, I don't know what I think," Susan despaired. Studying Marisa's face, she said, "You said there was a dog at Kim's place, that he barked at you?'

"That's right. Kim must have heard him and came back to the house."

When Susan said no more, Marisa expression tightened again. "I don't know where your sister is now. I don't particularly care, as long as she's not with my husband. It's quite possible she killed that man." With those words, Marisa opened the door of Susan's car and climbed out. Her high-heeled sandals made angry clicking sounds on the concrete as she hurried across the parking lot.

Halting beside a low, sports car, she unlocked the door and climbed in.

Susan watched as with tires squealing, the red Corvette swung out of the lot and onto the street.

Chapter 19

▼

The shadows were lengthening as Susan pulled her car to a halt in front of Harry's house. She unlocked the door and entered the living room, which was beginning to darken in the waning light. There was no sign of her uncle.

Moving about the kitchen as if she were in a trance, she began to prepare something to eat. Not because she was hungry, but because she needed something to do to keep from falling apart. When she'd seen Marisa drive away in the red Corvette, she had known that at least a portion of Marisa's story was true, that she had been at Kim's place.

Esther Helgeson's grandson claimed he had seen a red Corvette in Kim's driveway the day she was assaulted.

Dimly, Susan heard Harry's car enter the garage attached to the house. She turned as the door opened and he came into the kitchen. He looked as if he had aged ten years. His face was haggard and pale, his shoulders hunched.

"I stopped by Moe's bar for a beer...." His voice echoed his disbelief. "I heard about the dead man...."

Going over to him, Susan placed her arm around his neck and held on to him as though, by her embrace, she could keep out the evil that threatened. Then taking him by the hand, she urged him to sit down on the sofa.

"I have to tell you something. I can't keep it to myself any longer." Stressing that he must not disclose what she was about to relate to him, she told him about the attempted break-in being a hoax—according to Marisa. About Kyle's being at Kim's place. About the Markum's tangled lives.

Shaking his head, Harry rubbed his hand over his wrinkled face in a gesture of puzzlement and despair.

"Do you have any idea where Kim could have gone?" Susan asked him.

"Your sister never was much on tellin' me what she was up to. She was afraid I might mess up her plans."

"Whatever you did or tried to do was for her own good," Susan comforted.

"Unfortunately, she didn't see it that way. She thought my mission in life was to make things difficult for her. To spoil her fun."

A few minutes later, as Harry and Susan went through the motions of eating the salad and sandwiches she had prepared, they attempted to bolster each other's spirits. They tried to strengthen each other's belief there was a logical explanation for Kim's disappearance, and that she was innocent of any wrongdoing.

Where are you, Kim? Susan agonized. Kim wouldn't have killed someone unless she had been provoked. If she had killed in self-defense she wouldn't have had a reason to run away. It was all so strange. So confusing.

Susan remembered the shattered woman who had agonized over the loss of the husband she had adored. She recalled Marisa's accusations that Kim had fabricated the story of the burglary attempt. Once again Susan saw the still form of the dead man. She saw the huge figure that had confronted her on the beach looming in the darkness of the night. Whatever had happened to Kim, whatever was going on with her, Susan knew, had begun before her arrival. Was this the climax—the final chapter?

A short time later, when Harry opened the door in response to the ringing of the doorbell, Susan froze at the sight of Reid Elison. She rose slowly from the sofa where she had been sitting.

For a long moment, she was unable to speak. "Have you…did you…?"

Reid shook his head. "We haven't found out anything yet. I was passing the house and thought I'd stop in a minute to see if you had heard from Kim."

"We haven't heard a thing," Harry said. He invited Reid to be seated. "I'll get some coffee." He disappeared into the kitchen and reappeared a few minutes later with three cups of coffee on a tray.

When he handed a cup to Susan who had sat down on the sofa again, she held on to it with both hands as if it were an anchor that would prevent her from drowning in her fears.

"Have you talked to Kim's neighbor, Mrs. Helgeson?" she asked, her fingers clutching the coffee cup. "She lives near Kim's place. Maybe she saw or heard something."

"I talked to her, but she said she was in town all afternoon for the meeting of the Garden Club."

Harry asked Reid if he had learned the identity of the dead man.

"Not yet, but we will," was the answer.

Susan slumped against the back of the sofa and stared blankly into the cup she was holding. After a long moment, she sat up and placed it on the end table so hard that the dark liquid sloshed around the rim and spilled onto the table. "We have to find Kim." Their life together as *real sisters* had been short. They hadn't had a chance to really know each other. It couldn't end yet.

"We will find her," Reid assured Susan in a firm voice. "I can't promise more than that. We're checking every person and every place we can think of, asking all kinds of questions, but we're getting no answers."

Harry shot Susan a quick, darting look. For a minute, she was afraid he was going to tell Reid what she had told him in confidence. He seemed to be waiting, to have placed the weight of the burden on her shoulders.

For an instant, she, too, considered telling Reid what she had learned, and like Kim, let the chips fall where they would, but she caught herself. What had been going on in her sister's private life seemed too personal, too intimate, and too sordid to disclose to anyone outside the family. She wasn't ready to release the salacious details of her sister's love life as fodder for small town gossip.

Tomorrow—Susan vowed. Tomorrow, if nothing turned up, she would tell Reid about it. She had made a promise to Kyle and she must keep it, at least for the moment. But if anything could help Kim, anything at all, she wouldn't hesitate to use it. Promises could be retracted. Death could not be.

Harry was gone when Susan awakened the next morning. In a note he'd left on the table, he explained that although it was Saturday, he had to go to the office for several hours. What occurred in the lives of others, no matter how devastating, did not alter the course of the masses, Susan realized. They ate. They went to work. They made love.

In spite of the early hour, the day was already promising to be another hot one. The air was laden with humidity, the breeze non-existent. Frustrated and on edge, Susan despaired that she couldn't sit around and stare at the four walls. She had to do something or she would go out of her mind. It was apparent the sheriff's department hadn't found out anything. Reid would have called.

She had learned a long time ago that she couldn't depend on others. Her father hadn't defended her against her stepmother's tirades and false accusations toward her. After her divorce, the few friends she'd had were too involved in their own problems to concern themselves with hers. It was evident from Mark's phone call that in spite of the fact he'd said he had changed, his only concern had been with himself and what he wanted. He didn't realize or care about her needs or desires. And Gil—she wasn't certain where he stood beyond the fact that he had wanted to get her into his bed. The only person she could rely on, Susan knew, was herself.

She stroked her fingers thoughtfully across her chin. What could she do to find Kim? Maybe nothing, but she had to try. Perhaps if she went out to Kim's place—maybe something had been overlooked that would provide a clue to her whereabouts.

An hour later Susan sped toward Long Lake, wriggling ghost snakes of heat already rising from the pavement. The countryside was a hazy blue. In the distance, where the woods and the open spaces met, a mirage hung like a shimmering veil.

If she found out something derogatory about Kim—and that loomed as a possibility—Susan knew she would have to deal with it. There was no doubt in her mind that something strange was going on in Kim's life. With the murder and Kim's disappearance, and if Marisa had told the truth, the whole pattern of events had taken on another color. If Kim hadn't been the victim of an assault, as Marisa claimed, then she had to be the inventor of one. A schemer on her own.

Either Kim had been forcibly abducted, for what reason Susan couldn't comprehend, or she had disappeared of her own volition. Or had she been murdered, too, and her body disposed of? Was she lying alone and lifeless somewhere, her blood staining the ground beneath her?

Around and around the questions whirled, growing more virulent.

The possibility that Kim had gone off somewhere and was safe and sound had faded with each passing hour.

An examination of Kim's house might reveal something, Susan hoped, might bring the concept of her sister into sharper focus. She was searching, not only for evidence of the crime that had been committed, but also for clues to a life—Kim's life. Not only for what had happened to her and where she could be found, but what kind of person she really was.

Alongside Kim's wooded driveway, the sun had brought into blossom patches of wild flowers. The damp, musky scent of moist soil and growing greenery tingled in Susan's nostrils. In the area that wasn't shaded, the rustic texture of Kim's lake home was tinted in a rosy brown by the hard, hot light of the sun.

The blood on the flagstones had dried and was a dark stain on the blocks. The lawn had been carefully combed and photographed for evidence the previous afternoon, it's long grass trampled. Undoubtedly, the house had been searched, too. Susan wondered if the door was locked.

Stooping under the yellow ribbon that cordoned off the front yard, she walked up the steps and turned the knob. The door opened. Apparently the police had neglected to lock it. How Reid would accept what she was doing, Susan didn't dare think about. She could almost see his gray eyes snapping with reproach.

The inside of the house was just as it had been the day before. The partially eaten sandwich lay drying on the plate, the half-cup of black coffee alongside it. The house felt empty, like a hollow tomb. Reticently, disliking what she was doing, she crossed the living room and opened the drawer where the gun had been.

It was gone—she had known it would be. All she found in the drawer were several utility bills and a letter she had written to Kim months ago.

It came to Susan that the dead man—whose death had turned her world on end and was the reason for this search—had faded from the picture. It was as if he, as a real person, a victim, had lost his importance, and that she was searching for the answer to some other puzzle to which his death had been incidental. She saw him as a stranger who had unintentionally blundered across the twisted path that Kim traversed; someone who had inherently been plunged into death for a reason Susan could not fathom. Had he been murdered by the sister who's blood she shared? Then the vision disappeared, leaving Susan none the wiser.

At the sound of footfalls behind her she tensed, the fine hair on the nape of her neck stiffening. She whirled, her heart catching.

"Kim?" The word was a harsh cry.

Chapter 20

"What do you think you're doing?" Reid demanded sternly. "Don't you know you're not supposed to cross under the yellow police ribbon?"

Susan flushed under the intensity of his flint gray eyes. "I was looking—hoping to find something that would give me a clue to Kim's whereabouts."

"So you still think I'm a bumbling incompetent that can't find the nose on his face."

"It's not that," Susan denied quickly. "I thought that I might find something you had overlooked. What are you doing here?"

"I came back to give the place another going over."

"I'm closer to my sister," Susan pointed out. "Maybe I can find something that doesn't mean anything to you, but might be important."

Reid hesitated. "Are you sure you want to do this? That it isn't too much for you?"

"I'll be okay."

Reid released a reluctant sigh, as if he were uncertain if he were doing the right thing. "I'll look around in here. We searched the bedroom before, but you can go through Kim's personal things again if you want to."

"I'll do whatever it takes to find my sister."

Once again, the faint scent of Kim's light, summery perfume filled Susan's nostrils as she entered the bedroom. She felt strange, as if she were intruding in Kim's private life, a place where she had no business. She knew how Kim would react if she were aware of what was going on. Her dark eyes would snap, her lips tighten in annoyance.

"Stop playing detective," Kim had admonished. "I can take care of myself."

In this room, Kim and Brad had made love, Susan thought warily. In this room, Kim had cried out in the darkness at the loss of the man she loved so passionately. Undoubtedly, she and Kyle Markum had made love here, too.

Methodically, Susan searched the dresser drawers one by one, sorted through lingerie and odds and ends of clothing, but her efforts proved fruitless. Overcome with frustration, she shoved the last drawer shut. Eyes misting in disappointment, she rubbed her fingers across her brow in despair.

"Find anything?" Reid asked, poking his head into the room.

Lowering her hand, Susan took a deep breath, and pulled open the drawer again. "No, but I'm going to go over everything one more time. Maybe I missed something."

"I'll check the garage," Reid told her.

Once again, Susan thrust her hands under the assortment of clothing and lingerie that she found inside, stirring them about.

Then her fingers caught the edge of a small envelope. She removed it slowly, carefully from the drawer, as if she were removing a land mine. Unsure what she would find, she opened it. Inside were several snapshots of Kim and Brad. One was of them smiling happily on the beach. Another of them on the floor in front of the fireplace, probably taken with a time release camera. Susan's gaze swept over a snapshot of a group of men gathered around a race car. Brad was in the driver's seat, the others posed around him. She took the snapshot into the brighter light by the window and studied it closely.

On the side of the face of one of the men, she saw a small, white, puckered streak. As she stared at the photograph, Susan had the curious feeling of losing touch with Kim, like her sister was slipping away from her. That she, Susan, was being confronted with something strange, something more terrible than the actual death of the man on the flagstones—of the scar-faced man in the photo she was holding in her hand.

The dead man hadn't been a stranger to Kim. He hadn't been a burglar, or at least it didn't appear likely. He had been a friend or an acquaintance of Brad's, and he had been shot in the back.

At the sound of Reid's approaching footfall, Susan slipped the snapshot into her shirt pocket.

"Find anything?" he asked from the doorway.

"Nothing except some old snapshots of Kim and Brad." Susan slid the remaining pictures back into the envelope and returned it to the dresser drawer. She knew she had no business withholding evidence, but she didn't want to tell him what she had found or what she knew just yet.

"How about you?" she asked. "Did you find anything?"

Reid shook his head.

The frustration of the search and the humidity gave Susan an air of dishevelment. Short tendrils of brown hair clung to the nape of her neck, and her cheeks were flushed as she and Reid walked outside. The air was motionless, the sun a smoldering ball over the trees. It blazed downward, wilting the leaves, scorching the life out of everything within its reach.

When she opened the door of her car, a burst of hot air struck her in the face. The seat was searing to the touch as she slid onto it. A glance at her watch revealed it was almost noon. She had to find Harry and show him the snapshot. Perhaps he could put a name on the man with the scar.

As Susan rolled down the window, Reid leaned over and peered in at her. "It would be best if you left the investigating to the sheriff's department."

"I've got to do something. I can't sit around for weeks, maybe months...."

"Most cases aren't solved overnight. That only happens on television or in the movies."

Susan knew she wasn't being fair, but she couldn't sit back and wait for something else to happen. What if Kim wasn't found, just as the man who had assaulted her had not been found?

"This is a murder case," Reid stressed. "If your sister didn't kill that man, someone else did. You may be in putting yourself in danger. I don't need another victim."

"I can take care of myself." As she finished speaking, Susan recalled the times Kim had uttered those same words.

"I understand how you feel," Reid empathized. "But you can't go poking around on your own."

"I can't just sit around and twiddle my thumbs. Go on with my life as if nothing's happened."

"It would be a helleva lot better than messing around in a murder case—unless you want to end up dead, too."

"Don't be ridiculous!" Pushing back the damp hair from her brow, Susan switched on the ignition with a quick twist of her wrist. When the engine leapt to life, she shoved the shifting lever into gear and accelerated out of the yard.

She knew she was behaving badly, but she couldn't let Reid influence her. The idea that she was placing her life in jeopardy by trying to find Kim was absurd. And even if there were a chance that Reid was right, she couldn't allow fear to outweigh her responsibility or her loyalty to her sister. If she hadn't let Kim intimidate her, if she had insisted on staying with her sister no matter how much Kim protested, none of this would have happened.

So she thinks I'm incompetent, Reid thought as he watched Susan speed out of the driveway. Hell, he was beginning to think so himself. He shouldn't have come down on her so hard. But, Christ, he didn't want her getting her head blown off, too.

He climbed into the patrol car, yanked the door shut, and snapped on the seat belt. What had the guy been doing out here? He wondered as he looked across the lawn to the spot where the dead man had lain yesterday. How the hell had he gotten here? He hadn't dropped out of the sky.

Reid stroked his mustache thoughtfully, then jammed his fingers through his thick thatch of dark hair in frustration. Was he ever going to find the pieces to this damned puzzle?

He wondered if he had convinced Susan that she should keep her nose out of police business. Nice nose. Nice face. An okay lady. With a backbone malleable enough to bend, but wouldn't break.

He told himself to forget about Susan Edwards. *Think about murder. Go back to the beginning.*

Kim Hastings was assaulted. Her sister was attacked. By the same guy? Possibly.

Man is murdered on premises. By the same guy who assaulted and attacked the two women?

Chapter 21

Susan phoned the newspaper office as soon as she reached town and was told that Harry had gone to lunch. Minutes later, she was at Miller's Cafe, sliding onto the leather-bound seat across from him. Reaching into the pocket of her shirt, she pulled out the snapshot she had found in Kim's dresser.

Placing it on the table in front of him, she asked, "Do you know anyone in this picture besides Brad?"

He picked it up and held it at arm's length. Squinting, he growled, "I guess I'm gonna have to break down and buy me a new pair of specks. I can't see squat with these damned things."

Susan pointed a finger at the scar-faced man. "What about this guy?"

Harry's eyes pulled into narrowed slits as he studied the photo. "His name's Al Preston," Harry said as he lowered the picture.

"That's the dead man who was found at Kim's yesterday."

"What!" Harry exclaimed, his eyes widening in astonishment. "Where did you get this picture?"

Susan told him.

"What's a guy like Preston doin' at Kim's place?"

"So you know him?"

Again, Harry peered at the snapshot, studying it carefully. "I ran across this dude one night a month or so ago." He paused, his lined brow furrowing. "Come to think of it, it was about the time that thing happened to Kim—the break-in attempt that Marisa Markum told you was a hoax."

"Anyway," he continued. "Preston was at Moe's tyin' one on when I stopped in for a couple of beers after work. We struck up a conversation at the bar. He was really plowed. Kept cryin' in his beer about some big deal he'd been workin' was in danger of fallin' through. He swore, if it did, he was gonna get even with the person responsible."

Incredulity spread across Harry's face, like a light bulb being switched on. "Do you suppose this guy was out to Kim's askin' for a handout? From this picture, he musta been a friend of Brad's. Maybe he thought he'd replenish his empty pocketbook by givin' his old buddy's wife a sad song about being broke and starvin'."

"When he discovered there was no one home, maybe he thought he'd help himself," Susan conjectured. "If that's what he was doing and Kim caught him at it, wouldn't she have recognized him? If she didn't, would she have shot him and run away? No one would condemn her for protecting herself and her property from a thief."

Harry was thoughtful for a moment. "This guy was a petty hustler. Maybe he found Kim and Kyle Markum together, and was fixin' to commit a little blackmail."

Susan's brow knitted thoughtfully. Her uncle's tentative remark made sense. If Preston had found Kim alone and tried to coerce her, she might have blown her cool. She had a short fuse. If she were pushed, she might have lost control of her temper. But she wouldn't do something as drastic as kill him....

Or would she...?

Noticing that Harry was looking toward the entrance of the cafe, Susan's gaze followed his.

Arms laden with packages, Marisa Markum and another young woman were entering the restaurant. Eyes on an empty booth near the back, the two women made their way toward it.

"Hello, Marisa," Susan greeted in a low voice as they neared the table.

Marisa nodded tersely.

Uncertain why she was doing it, Susan picked up the snapshot from in front of her and held it up. "Do you know this man?" She pointed to Al Preston.

Halting, Marisa glanced at the photo. Then her face turned chalky white. "Of course not." Quickly, she turned and began to walk away, her hands clutching onto the packages in her arms.

Susan was behind her immediately. Placing her hand on Marisa's arm, she asked quietly, "What's the rush? You recognized him, didn't you?"

"No!" Marisa denied in a harsh hiss.

"This is no time for games," Susan rebuked.

Her expression stony and defiant, Marisa stood her ground, "I'm not the one who's playing games."

"This is important!" Susan stressed. "I need to find out if you know the man in this photo."

Marisa's mouth tightened. "I don't know anyone in the picture."

"I think you do. Perhaps you'd rather talk to Reid Elison."

Marisa attempted to jerk her arm from Susan's grasp, but Susan held on. She waited, her gaze fixed on Marisa's face.

The dark-haired woman stopped struggling. "Okay. It can't mean anything anyway. I saw that guy at Gil's place yesterday. I stopped out there right after I arrived home from visiting my parents, before I found you having your little t'ete-a-t'ete with my husband."

Susan stiffened, taken aback by Marisa's statement. "What was the guy doing out there?"

"How should I know? He entered the driveway as I was going out. The housekeeper was the only person I talked to. If Gil was home, I didn't see him. The only reason I was there was to pick up something I'd left there last week. Why are you asking all these questions?"

"The man with the scar is the person who was killed out at Kim's yesterday."

Marisa's fingers tightened around the packages she was holding. Green eyes blazing, she snapped, "How dare you try to involve me or my family in a murder your trampy sister probably committed! I'll deny everything I told you."

Susan flinched at Marisa's accusations. She could feel the dark-haired woman's anger. Her fear. If Gil or someone in his family were implicated in an unsavory murder case, Gil wouldn't be happy. But who would?

Gil could be a dangerous man when angered. Susan likened him to a wild animal that was prepared to pounce and tear at anyone who dared defy or cross him. She recalled the expression in his piercing blue eyes when he discovered she was Kim's sister.

"You said yesterday that Kyle had been at the plant," Marisa reminded Susan. "He couldn't have killed that man."

Empathy for the confused and frightened woman softened Susan's anger. In her fear, Marisa was concerned about the man she loved. And Kyle was innocent—unless he had lied about the time he'd left Kim's place. Unless he'd still been there when the man arrived. Unless the medical examiner had been wrong about the time the dead man had been killed.

Thanking Marisa for her help, Susan returned to the booth where Harry was sitting. Marisa joined her friend who had sat down in a booth and had witnessed the encounter in bewilderment.

"Well?" Harry said as Susan slid into the seat across from him. "What did she say?"

"She said the guy in the photo was out at Gil's place yesterday."

Harry exhaled a long gust of air through his mouth. "Holy Christ…this keeps gettin' weirder and weirder. You better stop messin' around in it. Go to Reid and tell him everything you know. This is work for the sheriff's department, not for amateurs. If Markum's involved in this—"

Susan flinched at Harry's words. Common sense told her that getting to the bottom of what had taken place at Kim's and her whereabouts took precedence over her feelings for Gil. Over Kim's reputation or any promise to Kyle she may have made. Matters were becoming more complicated by the minute. Chillingly so.

"You could get yourself killed," Harry warned. "Who knows who the hell's involved in this or why. Someone may be tryin' to cover up something. And I'm not referring to just the dead man on Kim's lawn."

A half-hour later, Susan was in the sheriff's office, standing in front of Reid's desk. She handed him the photo. "I found this at Kim's place this morning. It's a picture of the dead man. His name is Al Preston."

Reid gave the snapshot a quick glance, then returned it to Susan. "We know who he is. He hangs around the racetracks. He has a record of petty larceny, bookmaking, and extortion."

"I should have given the photo to you right away."

"That's right. You should have." Reid's gray eyes reprimanded her silently. "I know you're getting impatient with this thing. But you're not helping by withholding evidence or information. If we knew more about what's going on, we might be able to find your sister quicker."

He spoke brusquely, but not without understanding. Susan was relieved. She had expected him to be furious. She wouldn't have blamed him if he were.

After apologizing for what she had done, she told him everything she had learned. When she finished, Reid emitted a low whistle.

"Is that all this time?" His expression was stern as he looked at her.

Aware that she deserved his mistrust, color flooded over Susan's face. "That's all." Unable to meet his gaze, she lowered her head and stared down at the floor. "I'm sorry."

"I understand where you're coming from," he said, compassion evident beneath his stern exterior. "But next time, leave the detective work to me, okay? You could get yourself killed."

Susan gave him a weak smile.

After thanking her for coming to see him, Reid said, "Sorry if I was sharp with you. If we find out anything, I'll give you a call. I'm sure what you've told me is going to help."

Susan met his gaze. "I should have told you what I knew before."

Standing up, he walked around to the front of his desk. He made a motion as if to place his hands on her shoulders, then drew back. "I know this isn't easy for you."

She wanted him to tell her that none of this was taking place, that it was all a bad dream, and she would wake up any second. "Are you going to question Gil Markum?"

"I'm on my way."

"I want to go with you." She had to know if Gil were involved in this.

"Sorry. This is official business."

Her face stony with stubbornness, Susan pointed to the nameplate on his desk. "That says you're Chief Deputy. Surely you can bend the rules a little. This isn't Phoenix. Who'll know? Who'll care?"

He hesitated, but Susan's gaze was unwavering. "All right," he growled. "I suppose I'd better take you along, or you'll go out there on your own."

Reaching for the telephone on his desk, he punched in some numbers and asked for Gil. After listening for a moment, he thanked whomever he had spoken to, and hung up the receiver. "The receptionist at the plant says Gil's taking the afternoon off. Maybe he's at home."

A short time later, Gil opened the door at his spacious lake home in response to Reid's ring.

Gil's eyes widened at the sight of Susan, then shifted his gaze to Reid. "What can I do for the two of you?"

"You can answer a few questions," Reid told him.

Gil's huge frame stiffened. "What about?"

"Can we discuss this inside?" Reid asked.

Gil glanced at his watch. "You'll have to make it brief. I'm on my way to the Club for a round of golf with some friends." Stepping back, he motioned for Susan and Reid to enter.

As he led the way into the living room and invited them to be seated on the black leather couch, Susan was once again in awe of the ambiance, subdued by the intimidation it seemed to exude. The memory of the time she and Gil had spent together flooded into her mind; his touch, his kisses. Cheeks warming, she shifted uncomfortably as Gil stood in front of them, his hands in the pockets of his trousers. "Can I get you a drink?" he asked.

"No, thank you," Susan and Reid replied in unison.

Gil sat down on a deep-cushioned chair across from them. "It isn't often I receive a visit from a deputy sheriff. What's this about? Did I drive too fast or go through a stop sign? I've been known to do that a time or two." A crooked smile elevated the corner of his mouth.

"Do you know a man by the name of Al Preston?" Reid asked.

Gil's heavy dark brows knitted thoughtfully. "I don't believe so. Why?"

"He's the guy who was killed out at the Hastings' place yesterday."

Gil looked over at Susan. "So that's why you're here. There's been a lot going on out there, hasn't there?" His tone was wry, almost accusatory.

"Your daughter-in-law said Preston was out here yesterday," Reid told the white-haired man. "Just a short time before he was killed."

Stiffening, Gil leaned forward in his chair. His eyes were sharp with anger. "You've been questioning Marisa?"

"I showed her a picture with Preston in it," Susan explained hastily. "She said she saw him turn into your driveway yesterday."

"What!" Gil exclaimed in disbelief. "She said she saw him *here?*"

Susan nodded weakly, intimidated by the fury in his eyes.

"No way." Gil's strong jaw jutted out. "I was with you and Harry at the Country Club yesterday, remember?'

"Yes," Susan acknowledged. "A short time before I went out to Kim's and found the dead man…." She broke off, chilled by the memory of the bloodied body on the lawn.

"Surely you don't think I had anything to do with that!" Gil demanded. "Did Marisa say she saw me with that guy?"

"She said Preston entered the driveway as she was leaving."

"I've never seen nor heard of Preston or whatever the hell his name is," Gil maintained staunchly.

"Where were you yesterday morning?" Reid asked, obviously not intimidated by the wealthy businessman.

"I was at the office. What's that got to do with anything?"

"Perhaps you'd like to call your attorney," Reid suggested.

"What the hell for? I've got nothing to hide. I said I don't know the guy, didn't I?"

"What time did you leave your office yesterday?" Reid asked.

"Close to noon. I had several errands to run before I came home. I had a two o'clock appointment for the interview with Harry at the Club. I was a few minutes late. I took a walk around the grounds when I got home and lost track of time."

When Reid remained silent, Gil asked if he would like to question his housekeeper. "She'll tell you I was here."

"Please," Reid urged.

The white-haired man excused himself and returned a few minutes later with a plump, middle-aged woman he introduced as Olga. She cast a darting glance at Susan, then stood waiting. When Reid questioned her, she said she had talked to Marisa, but hadn't see anyone else except for Gil whom she'd noticed walking across the back yard at twelve thirty or so.

"Was Mr. Markum alone?" Reid asked.

The stoic-faced housekeeper nodded. "He was."

"Are you sure about that?"

"Positive," Olga responded. Her back was erect. Her chin jutted out.

Rising, Reid thanked Gil and Olga for their time and cooperation.

"What do you think?" Susan asked as he drove away from Gil's place. "Was he telling the truth?"

"The housekeeper said Gil was home, and that she didn't see Preston." If he had any doubts or suspicions, Reid kept them to himself. "You don't want him to be involved, do you, Susan?"

A wash of color spread over her face. "Why should someone like Gil Markum have anything to do with a creep like Al Preston?"

"That's what I'd like to know."

Susan spent the rest of the afternoon pacing the floor of Harry's living room and drinking black coffee, until she could almost hear it sloshing inside her as she moved about.

Over and over, the same questions churned in her head, until she felt disembodied, disconnected from herself. What had Preston been doing at Kim's? Why had he been killed and who had killed him? Where was Kim and why had she run away? *Had* she run away, or had something happened to her? Susan didn't want to think about that.

The shrill ringing of the telephone made her jump, like a shock from a live wire. Pulse quickening, she held back for a moment, afraid to lift the receiver. Giving her watch a quick glance, she noted that it was four-thirty, exactly twenty-four hours since she had discovered the dead man on Kim's doorstep.

She picked up the receiver.

It was Reid. "We've found your sister."

Chapter 22

▼

Tentacles of dread wrapped themselves around Susan, rendering her momentarily speechless. Had Reid placed Kim under arrest? Was she in jail? "Where is she? Is she...."

"She's in the hospital. She's in a coma."

"A coma!" Susan gasped. "What happened to her? Where has she been?"

"Apparently her car went off the road on a sharp curve and plunged down an embankment a mile east of her place. A motorist found her. Undoubtedly, she's been there since yesterday, but no one noticed the car because of all the brush and trees."

"I've got to go to her!" Susan cried.

"You're in no shape to drive. I'll come over and pick you up. I'll call Harry. He can meet us at the hospital."

Enroute to the hospital, dimly, through the roaring in her ears and a mind that was numb, Susan heard Reid explain how Kim's car had gotten hung up on a large rock halfway down a steep embankment, preventing it from plunging into Long Lake.

As they walked down the corridor toward the Intensive Care Unit, Harry caught up with them, limping and short of breath.

"Looks like my marathon days are over," he panted.

A sign on the door to the ICU indicated, "No Admittance Without Permission."

Susan tapped on the door.

A stern-faced nurse whose nametag revealed she was "Anne Thomas RN" opened it. After identifying themselves as family, Susan and Harry were allowed inside the room. Reid waited outside in the corridor.

There were four beds inside the ICU. The heavy, floor length sheets that separated them were attached to metal tracks on the ceiling, and were pushed aside, revealing that three of the beds were empty. Anne Thomas led Susan and Harry over to the fourth one.

Susan froze at the sight of the lifeless form underneath the sterile white sheets. Drawing in her breath, she forced herself to look at the battered and bandaged, unrecognizable body of her sister. An IV was connected to a metal stand, the tube inserted into Kim's limp arm, a colorless fluid flowing through it. Machines with electrical wires and winking and blinking red lights stood at the head of the bed.

"You can see her for just a few minutes," the gray-haired nurse cautioned.

Why are all these people hovering around me, whispering as people do around those on their deathbeds? Kim wondered. *I can't make out a word they're saying.*

They've come and gone, examined and did things to me. Actually, I'm not sure they've really been here, and aren't just hovering, insubstantial shadows.

Like the shadows, I'm here too, but not really. I'm floating in space most of the time, out of my body. If only I could hear and understand what they're saying maybe I'd know where I am. Susan just walked in the door. I know it's her. I can see her clearly. She's substance, and she's looking at me. There's an expression of horror on her face. I'd like to tell her I'm okay, that I'm glad to see her, but I can't seem to move. I treated her like shit. It wasn't because I wanted to; it was because I had to. For all the good it did. I wouldn't blame her if she never spoke to me again.

There's someone else with her. I can see a black outline, nothing more.

"Kim?" Susan said softly. "Can you hear me? It's Susan...." She placed her hand on Kim's limp arm.

I can hear her, understand her words. I can feel her hand is on my arm. I'm not sure which one. I feel better that she's here, that she cares about me. I don't deserve her.

"I hope you can hear me, Kim."

I want to tell her I can hear, but my face hurts and my brain won't work. She's standing beside me, talking slowly and quietly, never letting go of my hand. How I wish I could at least squeeze her fingers.

"We've been worried about you. We've been looking all over for you," Susan is saying now.

"I've been here at home all day. I've had..." *Why won't my mouth work?*

She's still staring down at me. I wish I could give her some sort of sign, but I can't. I'm just a blob lying here. It feels as if I'm in bed—in my own bed? No, it's not. I can tell. But where am I? How did I get to this place, whatever it is?

It stinks. Smells like a hospital.

"You're lucky your car didn't fall all the way down the cliff."

What's she talking about? I didn't fall off any cliff. I never left my place. It doesn't make any sense. Nothing happening right now makes any sense. This place. This smell. All these people hovering over me.

The other shadowy figure is closer to me now, in my line of vision. It's Uncle Harry. He's patting my hand. Good old Uncle Harry.

"Glad you're still with us, kid."

He looks worried. But then he's always pissed with me about one thing or another. One of these days he's going to keel over from a heart attack because of all his stewing. But I'm glad he's here, too. I never thought I'd feel that way, but strangely, I do. Truthfully, he's a pretty nice guy. He just kept getting in my way when I was younger. Now he and Susan are my only connection to what is real, to what this is all about.

He's saying something to her now. I can't make it out, but there's concern on both their faces.

God, I hurt. I need a pain pill. I hope they don't leave me here alone.

"Your sister's unconscious," Anne Thomas said as Susan clung to Kim's hand.

"How badly has she been hurt?" Susan asked.

"You'll have to talk to her doctor about that. But she's a very sick girl." Leaving Susan and Harry alone, the nurse moved over to the desk and sat down.

Susan reached for Harry's hand and held on to it, fought back the fears that threatened to overwhelm her.

Kim's eyes were closed. The portion of her face that wasn't swathed in bandages, was blue and swollen. The pale hair above her bandaged forehead was matted and dotted with small particles of dried blood. Her breathing was shallow and ragged.

As though they were one, Susan felt her sister's pain filling her own body. It didn't matter what Kim had done. The important thing was that she would be all right.

As she looked down at the battered and broken body on the bed, Susan was overwhelmed with a sense of failure. She should have been able to prevent this from occurring. Harry had asked her to see if she could help her sister. She had failed miserably. If she had gone out to Kim's place earlier instead of dragging her feet, she might have prevented this from happening. Susan choked back the tears that blurred her vision.

"Oh, God!" she whispered, overcome with grief. "Why did this have to happen to Kim?"

Susan felt her uncle's arm go around her shoulder.

"It's not your fault," he comforted, as if he could read her mind. "Only Kim knows why and how this happened."

Ten minutes later, as Susan, Harry, and Reid walked out of the hospital together, Reid told Susan he would talk to her tomorrow. That he hoped Kim improved soon so he could get a statement from her and clear things up.

After they bid him goodbye and were walking across the hospital's parking lot, a pale and obviously shaken Harry suggested they go to the Bayside for something to eat before they went home. "We could go to Miller's, but they don't have set-ups," he said. "I could use a drink."

Susan knew she couldn't eat anything, and having a drink seemed inappropriate, almost sacrilegious with Kim lying near death. But she dreaded going back to Harry's big house with its empty rooms and hollow silence. Falling asleep later, she knew, would be impossible without sedation.

Fifteen minutes later, as they made their way toward a table at The Bayside, Susan noticed the Markums—Kyle, Marisa, and Gil—seated at a table with tall, frosted drinks in front of them.

As she approached their table, Kyle's gaze lifted and met Susan's.

"Something's happened." His voice was toneless. "I can tell by the expression on your face."

Susan halted beside his table. "Kim's been found. She's in the hospital."

Kyle's face was the color of ashes.

Gil, too, was suddenly white-faced. "What happened? How is she?"

"She's in intensive care," Susan answered. "Her car went over the side of a cliff. We won't know what happened until she regains consciousness."

Kyle's eyes were swimming with anguish. Susan recognized his fear, his apprehension, for she was experiencing similar misgivings.

"Where are you going?" Gil asked as Kyle rose to his feet.

Kim's accident, her discovery, seemed to be effecting Gil as much as it did Kyle. White lines had formed around Gil's mouth, and his jaw was tense. As she studied him, Susan tried to get the measure of the man who so utterly fascinated her. They had almost made love; he had changed from charming and flirtatious to distant, almost hostile, when he discovered that Kim was her sister.

"I'm going to the hospital," Kyle told his father.

"Only members of the family are allowed to see someone in ICU," Gil stressed. "Didn't you hear what Susan said? Her sister is unconscious."

"I don't care. I'm going there anyway. At least I'll be there if Kim needs me."

If he had been unaware that his father and his wife knew of his affair with Kim, it was out in the open now. Kyle didn't seem to notice or care.

"Sit down and get a hold of yourself." The nostrils of Gil's hawkish nose were pinched in disapproval. "It's not going to do you any good to go to the hospital."

Slowly, obediently, Kyle lowered himself onto his chair. The glow of the supper club's interior lighting tinted his beard and sandy hair a sickly yellow. Fastening the fingers of one hand around the glass in front of him, he gazed down into its contents. The fingers on his other hand were pressed against his temples, as if to hold up his bowed head.

Marisa, too, was clinging onto her glass as if it were a protective talisman, as if she were holding onto life itself. Despair dulled her green eyes. Hands trembling slightly, she lifted her drink to her lips. Vermouth splashed out of the glass, spilled onto the pale embroidery of her white linen dress. It made a red stain like blood, but she didn't seem to notice.

Moving closer to Kyle, she placed her hand on his arm. He sat rigid and motionless, seemingly totally unmindful of her, as if she were a stranger or not really there at all.

Then, lifting his head, Kyle looked across the table at his father with dark reproach in his eyes. Shoving back his glass, he leapt to his feet. Ignoring Marisa's hold on his arm, he moved toward the exit with long, sure strides.

Gil stood up quickly, his face reddening in anger. "Where are you going?" he called after Kyle.

Shoving open the door, Kyle hurried out without a backward look.

Gil's angry gaze followed his son for several minutes. Then he turned to look at Susan for a brief moment. His face was impassive, like a mask of hardwood. But his eyes were like burning coals, his nostrils flaring in a menacing manner. Then he looked away, and dashed after his son.

Susan felt Harry's hand on her arm. "Let's sit down and have our drink. I've had about all I can handle for one day."

Susan looked over at Marisa who sat alone at the table. "Are you all right? Can I do anything...."

Marisa stared toward the exit, her countenance drained of emotion, as if she were watching her world end and she knew she could do nothing about it. As if she felt Susan's gaze on her, she turned. "I hope your sister never regains consciousness."

Later that night, sleep eluded Susan, as she had known it would. She tossed from side to side, wondering what had happened the afternoon Preston was killed, and why Kim had left home in her car. Had she shot him, panicked and fled, and in her haste, ran off the embankment? It seemed a logical explanation. But why had she killed him—if she had—and why had Preston been there in the first place?

Then a thought so horrendous flashed into Susan's mind that it took her breath away. What if Kim didn't come out of her coma? What if—

No! She must not think such things! She must thrust them away, as though by not voicing the possibility, denying its very existence, she could alter it.

But she couldn't put the picture of Marisa's face, when Kyle stated he was going to the hospital to be with Kim, out of her mind. Marisa had been crushed, utterly devastated. In her face, too, had been a blazing hatred, hatred for the woman who had taken her man from her.

Susan thoughts turned to Gil. Once again she wondered why he was suddenly treating her as if she were a stranger, as if there had been nothing between them. Or had she just imagined that there had been?

Turning back onto her left side, she looked out the window next to her bed. Heat lightning flashed across the darkened sky, lighting up the room like mid-day at times. Heat lightning, she knew, indicated the presence of a storm, its thunder too distant to hear. Sometime later, sleep captured her, but it was not without dreams. She was running, running, being chased by a huge faceless figure in black. The breath tore at her chest. Then her legs gave out beneath her, and she stumbled. Huge fingers tightened around her throat. She bolted upright in bed, a silent scream on her lips.

"Your sister is seriously injured," Dr. Weston explained the next morning when Susan and her uncle confronted him in the corridor as he was making his rounds. "Besides facial bruises and head injuries, she has extensive internal injuries. A ruptured spleen, kidney damage, broken hips and pelvis, fractured ribs—you name it, she's got it. It's a miracle she's alive."

"Do you have any idea when she'll regain consciousness?" Harry asked.

Dr. Weston's eyes were grave behind his dark-rimmed glasses. "We'll have to wait and see. Everything that can be done for her is being done."

Minutes later, as Susan and Harry approached the ICU, Susan was surprised to see Kyle Markum pacing back and forth in the hallway, an expression of anger and frustration on his bearded face.

"I've been trying to talk Old Stone Face into letting me in to see Kim, but she keeps refusing," Kyle said.

"I assume you're referring to Nurse Thomas," Susan said. "I'll talk to her."

Opening the door of the ICU, Susan peered inside. Spotting Nurse Thomas sitting at the desk, she asked if Kyle could come in for a minute or two.

The nurse shook her head. "Ms. Hastings is in a coma."

"I won't disturb her," Kyle promised from behind Susan. "I just want to see her."

"Only family members are permitted to visit patients in ICU," Anne Thomas stressed.

"I'm Kyle Markum. I'm a close friend," Kyle emphasized. "I know it would mean a great deal to Ms Hastings if she knew I've been in to see her."

The stern-faced nurse's eyes wavered. "Markum?" she repeated with a frown. "All right. You can go in, but only for a few minutes."

'Markum,' was the magic word, Susan thought as she and Harry waited in the hallway. The name obviously carried a lot of weight.

When he came out several minutes later, Kyle was white-faced, his shoulders hunched in despair. "My God..." He broke off, overcome with emotion.

Although she had been uncertain how she felt toward him before, Susan identified with him now, with the pain he was experiencing. She placed a comforting hand on his arm.

Closing his eyes, Kyle rubbed his hand across his bearded face, as if to erase what he had seen. Her hand on his arm, Susan guided him into the waiting room. He dropped onto a chair, legs apart, elbows resting on his thighs, supporting his bowed head. After several minutes, with an effort, he pulled himself erect.

"What in God's name happened out there?" he anguished.

"I wish I knew."

"I love her so much. My life's meaningless without her."

Susan placed her hand over Kyle's. Having a sister had given her a sense of identity, a feeling of belonging to a family in spite of the distance that had existed between during their adolescence. Blood could not be changed or altered. Somehow, she had managed to stumble through life so far, slipped through the layers leaving little evidence she'd been there. But this—this was something she couldn't hide from. It was far more devastating than anything she'd experienced before.

A few minutes later, after Kyle had composed himself, he told Susan he had to go. Accompanied by her uncle who had waited in the corridor while she comforted Kyle, Susan returned to the Intensive Care Unit.

She could scarcely bear to look at Kim's mutilated and swollen features, at her broken body. Gently, she stroked her sister's matted hair with the tips of her fingers. Kim was the one being left in the world she shared blood ties with. In spite of their differences, they were products of the same seed, the same womb. Those ties, Susan realized, could not be severed without losing a part of herself.

She's here again...my sister. Harry's here, too. I must really be in bad shape. Susan is holding my hand like before. Was it this morning when they were here? I have no sense of time at all; it has no meaning to me. The touch of my sister's hand is so comforting. I know she's here, that I'm not imagining it. I don't want to lose my brain...what's left of it...the way I've lost the rest of me. The way I've lost my sense of right and wrong. Oh, Lord, if Aunt Maggie knew what I've been up to....

Those other white, shadowy figures have been in here, too, bustling about, hovering over me, but they're gone now.

I want to cry with the sheer joy of seeing my sister, of hearing her voice, but I don't know if my body can feel, if it's capable of making noises or producing tears.

I want to ask her who found me and if anyone else was there at my house. No, of course they wouldn't be. They would have gotten the hell out of there—both of them.

"I don't know if you can hear me or not," Susan said. "I hope you can. Harry and I are here for you. Can you tell us what happened, Kim?"

What happened? I'm not sure. My head hurts! I keep trying to remember, but the messages don't seem to be reaching my brain.

No, wait...it's coming back...

I feel the pain of hard steel smashing against my head. Again and again. I feel my knees buckling.

Please, someone, help me! Oh, God! Oh God.... Susan...!

She can't hear me.

My mouth still isn't working. My words are bouncing around in my head like marbles.

"Tell us about the man outside your house," Susan implored. "Who shot him?"

Nobody shot anyone. I wanted to. Tried to. Someone stopped me. Or did they? Oh, God, why can't I remember?

"Tell me what happened, Kim. We'll get through this together."

Susan is leaning closer to me. I can feel the soft touch of her breath on my skin. I know she won't understand what's been going on with me. I'm not like her. I'm the eye for an eye type. But Lord, look where it's gotten me!

Susan must be like our mother, the mother I never knew. The mother who died because of me, that I killed. God I hope Susan can find it in her heart to forgive me, to understand why I've been doing what I have. That I'm a thief. That I wanted someone dead. Maybe made it happen.

He was a bastard. He wouldn't leave me alone. He tricked me. I had to do something. And now I'm here—in this place, hurting like hell, probably dying, by the look on everyone's face.

"Hang in there, Kimberly Joy," Susan prayed through misty eyes. "Don't lose your fighting spirit now."

Kim moaned and began to stir. Slowly, she moved her head from side to side on the pillow. "Give me the gun!" She cried out in a hoarse, grating voice.

Quickly, Susan took her hand. "Kim, it's Susan. It's all right."

"Please...." Kim whispered between bruised and swollen lips. "Don't hit me...."

"Who hit you?" Susan pleaded softly. "Who did this to you?"

Anne Thomas stood up from her chair alongside the desk and came over to Kim's bedside. "You'll have to leave now," she said to Susan.

"No, please," Susan pleaded. "Just a few more minutes."

"Sorry."

"Kim may be able to tell me what happened to her."

"She's delirious," Anne Thomas declared. "She doesn't know what she's saying."

Taking Susan's arm and motioning to Harry, the nurse steered them toward the door. "Ms. Hastings is a very sick girl. She can't tolerate anymore disturbance."

Filled with dismay, Susan and Harry took the elevator down to the lobby. As they walked out of the hospital, they met a uniformed Reid Elison coming toward them.

"How's your sister?" he asked as he halted beside them.

Throat constricting, Susan shook her head. "Not very good, I'm afraid. A few minutes ago, Kim cried out for someone to stop hitting her. When I tried to find out what she was talking about, her nurse ordered us out of the room. She said Kim was delirious."

"I'm sorry," Reid sympathized.

"Sounds as if Preston beat her," Harry conjectured. "She must have shot him in self defense, panicked, and ran away. She was driving too fast and ran off the cliff."

"That's possible," Reid concurred. "She could have received some of those bruises before her car went over the cliff. I was hoping her condition had improved so I could question her. Guess I'll have to wait a little longer, until she gets better."

"*If* she gets better," Susan said grimly.

Chapter 23

The realization of the words she had uttered, what she'd been thinking, horrified Susan. Her head reeled. White blotches burst at the corner of her vision, threatening to occlude everything around her.

Reaching out quickly, Reid took hold of her arm. "Are you okay?"

"I..." Susan rubbed her fingertips across her brow. "I felt a little dizzy for a moment. I'll be all right...."

"Are you sure?" Harry asked, his eyes filled with concern.

Pulling back her shoulders, Susan inhaled deeply, filling her lungs with fresh air. "I'm fine."

"You don't look fine," her uncle contradicted.

"How about a cup of coffee?" Reid suggested, still holding onto her arm. "There's a small coffee shop down the street that's open on Sunday. My patrol car's in the parking lot." He looked at Harry, including the older man in his invitation.

"You two go ahead," Harry urged. "I think I'll go home."

Placing his hand on Susan's elbow, Reid guided her across the paved lot to the black and white patrol car. "Have you eaten today?" he asked.

"I'm not hungry." Concern for her sister had robbed her of an appetite. Susan stood by until Reid opened the patrol car, then climbed in and fastened her seat belt. "Are you on duty today, too?"

Reid slid onto the seat beside her. "I don't mind. I have nothing better to do."

He had nothing better to do; what else is there to do? Kim had asked when Susan discovered her wearing a robe and her hair tangled from sleep in the middle of the afternoon. Why didn't these people get a life? Susan grimaced at the irony in her thoughts. Who was she to criticize others when her own life was in shambles?

"Did you get any sleep last night?" Reid asked.

"Not much." Nothing that had happened since her arrival in Lake Center made sense to her. The lack of reason ignited fearful questions that had denied her of sleep. When she had woken up, she was lying crossways in bed.

Opening the door that led into a small cafe which contained a half dozen booths and a horseshoe counter with worn leather stools, Reid followed as Susan walked over to a corner booth and sat down. When the waitress, who was wearing a mini skirt and had a small tattoo on her arm, placed menus in front of them, Susan didn't bother to open hers. "Just a cup of black coffee, please."

Reid handed the menu to the waitress. "I'll have a ham sandwich. Bring one for the lady, too."

When the waitress placed the coffee in front of her, Susan took a swallow to lessen the tightness that had formed in her throat. However this nightmare ended, she would be grateful to Reid. In the period of a few days, she had been assaulted, found a dead man, and almost lost her sister. Reid's calming demeanor and his reassurances had helped her maintain her sanity and made her feel as if she weren't alone.

As she studied him, she could not help but admire the strong, rugged profile that was crowned by a tumble of dark hair. He was an attractive man, she concluded. But it wasn't his looks that drew her to him, that softened her dislike toward him. There was a special concern in his eyes that made her feel he truly cared about her welfare.

"Mark called me the other day." She wasn't sure why she had brought up the subject.

His gaze fixed on her face; Reid waited for her to go on.

"He wanted to know when I'm coming out to LA."

Reid took a swallow of coffee, then set down the cup carefully. "What did you tell him?"

The memory of how she had stood up to her ex-husband brought a smile to her lips. "That I'd let him know."

Mark had taken over her life so completely when they had been married, had denied her of an identity, that she was still searching for who she was. He had dominated her life so that she had almost lost the ability to think and do for herself. Even now, she often found herself procrastinating, expecting a decision to be made for her instead of making it herself. As for her feelings toward Gil, his presence wasn't like any part of her real world, but a separate chapter onto itself.

"I'm not free to go anywhere or do anything until Kim is better," Susan told Reid, as if to justify her need to stay in Lake Center. Reality descended on her once again, blanketing her with fear and apprehension.

She waited as the waitress placed the ham sandwiches on the table and refilled the coffee cups. "Have you talked to Marisa?"

Reid nodded, his mouth twisting in a wry smile. "It seems she was mistaken about seeing Preston at Gil's place. She now says the man she saw turned around at the entrance to Gil's driveway and left without stopping."

Susan gasped in disbelief. "That's not what she told me."

"I can't accuse her of lying unless I have proof Preston was there." Reid was thoughtful for a moment. "The wallet and a gun were found in your sister's car. More than likely, when we get the ballistics report, it will show it's the gun that killed Preston."

Susan felt as if she were about to be swallowed up by the tiled floor beneath her feet. "I don't believe Kim killed that man."

"You've got to prepare yourself for the probability that, for whatever reason, she's guilty."

"That man was shot in the back. Surely you don't believe Kim would do something so cold blooded."

"I'm an officer of the law," Reid reminded her in measured tones. "No matter what I feel personally, I have to be objective, to consider all the possibilities."

"I realize that." Despair clutching at her once again, Susan released a weighty breath. "I guess I want someone to assure me that everything is going to be all right. That it isn't as bad as it appears to be."

Reid's eyes were filled with compassion as he looked at her. "I hate to see you so torn apart like this."

"How do you expect me to feel?" Susan anguished. "I can't abandon my sister because she may have done something wrong. She's a part of me. I can't just walk away—amputate her from my life."

"I understand where you're coming from. I've come to know you well enough to realize that you wouldn't abandon someone in trouble. But I think you've allowed yourself to become too close, too personally involved in this thing."

"How can I help but be personally involved? Kim is my sister."

"I'm not condemning you. We all tend to overlook the imperfections in those we love. I'm just as guilty of that as you are."

"Maybe it's because we realize we have some of those imperfections ourselves," Susan philosophized wearily.

"Probably."

"I'm sorry," Susan said. "I didn't mean to come down on you so hard. It's just that all of this…." She gestured helplessly. She was nearly at the end of her rope. It was all so frustrating, so confusing. So horrifying. Reid deserved her cooperation, not her disdain or criticism. It wasn't his fault that he had come up empty-handed at every turn. If there had been no rape or burglary attempt, as Marisa claimed, it was no wonder his investigation hadn't turned up anything.

Susan took a bite of her sandwich. It tasted like cardboard and she took a swallow of coffee to wash it down. "Have you found out anymore about Preston?"

"I've been asking around, but no one seems to know anything about the guy. The bartender at Moe's Bar, where Harry said he ran into Preston, couldn't remember anything in particular about him, except that he'd been in there a few times."

Susan placed her hands in her lap. "What I can't figure out is why Preston went out to Kim's place. What kind of business could she have with a guy like that, even if he'd been a friend of Brad's? According to Harry, Preston was a slime ball."

"An apt description," Reid growled.

"Maybe Marisa was lying and Kim really was assaulted—by Preston," Susan conjectured. "Maybe he came back, for whatever reason, to do it again. That's what Kim was afraid of and the reason she had the gun."

"It's possible. But what about the red Corvette Esther Helgeson's grandson saw in Kim's driveway?"

"It indicates that at least part of Marisa's story is true, that she was there," Susan granted. "Unless there's more than one red Corvette in the area, or there was at that time."

"It's conceivable, but unlikely."

"Mrs. Helgeson's grandson said he saw a red Corvette in Kim's driveway just like his friend's uncle owns."

"The only 'Vette I've seen in the area is Marisa's." Reid paused reflectively. "I talked to some people who live a ways down from Kim's place. One of them remembered hearing a shot the afternoon Preston was killed. The person thought it was kids hunting squirrels in the woods."

Taking a steadying breath, Susan pressed her fingers against her eyelids. What else would happen before this was over?

Were there too many pieces to the puzzle or not enough?

Chapter 24

Susan looked up as Kyle pulled his car alongside her Skyhawk in the hospital parking lot. The temperature had dropped from the previous days', and a light breeze brushed against her face. "How's Kim?" he called out as he braked to a halt.

"She's still in a coma." Standing beside her car, Susan reached in her handbag for the keys. She had come back to the hospital at five to check on Kim's condition and to bring her some flowers.

"What does the doctor say?" Kyle's bearded face held a haunted look, and there was a bleakness in his eyes.

"He said that everything possible is being done for her, that we'll have to wait and see." Susan couldn't keep the dejection out of her voice.

Kyle reached over to the passenger's side of his car and pushed open the door. "Have you got a few minutes?" When Susan slid in beside him, Kyle said, "I think we should find another doctor. I know a specialist."

Susan gave him a weak but grateful smile. "I don't know if a specialist will be of much help. There's only so much that can be done for someone in Kim's condition. It's up to a higher power...." Susan blinked back the tears that welled up in her eyes.

"Kim seemed to come out of her coma when Harry and I were in to see her this morning," Susan went on. "She said some things, but her nurse insisted that she was delirious and didn't know what she was saying."

"Did she say what happened to her?" Kyle asked.

"By what she said, it sounded as if someone took the gun away from her and beat her with it."

"Preston!" Kyle spat out the name. "It had to have been Preston."

"It appears that way. But then who killed *him?*" Susan repeated Harry's hypothesis that Kim shot Preston in self-defense, panicked and ran away. Driving too fast, she lost control of her car on the winding road and plunged over the cliff.

"The bastard!" Kyle slammed his hand against the steering wheel. "If Preston weren't dead already, I'd kill him with my bare hands."

"Did Kim ever mention his name to you?"

Kyle shook his head thoughtfully. "Not that I can recall."

The purr of a powerful automobile engine filled Susan's ears, interrupting the conversation. Her heartbeat quickened as a familiar white Lincoln pulled alongside Kyle's convertible.

"I figured I'd find you here," Gil growled, his taut countenance reflecting his disapproval of his son.

Kyle's gaze, as he peered at his father, was unwavering. "If you think you're going to stop me from seeing Kim, forget it."

"You're a damned fool."

"Is that what you drove in here to tell me?" Kyle asked.

"I saw your car from the street as I was passing by. I've invited Marisa's parents to have dinner with me tonight. I'd like for you and Marisa to join us. You do know her parents are in town, don't you? I think, for everyone's sake, you should at least act like a happily married man."

Kyle chortled. "Act like a happily married man? That's all my marriage has ever been—a pretense. When Kim recovers, I'm getting a divorce."

Gil's blue eyes were glistening like ice chips. "Are you forgetting who gets us the majority of our contracts?"

"That's all that matters to you, isn't it," Kyle mocked bitterly. "The damned business. The fact that the woman I love may not live means nothing to you at all."

Gil turned to Susan, his anger fading slightly. "From what I hear, your sister is still in serious condition. Has she come out of her coma yet?"

When Susan shook her head, he asked, "Does her doctor hold out any hope that she will?"

"He doesn't know."

Gil focused his attention on Kyle again. "I'll pick you and Marisa up in an hour."

Nodding at Susan, he shifted the Lincoln into reverse, then swung out of the parking lot, the car's powerful engine roaring.

In spite of the events of the last several days and his peculiar behavior toward her at the Country Club, Susan still felt an attraction for the wealthy businessman. There was something about him—his strength, the aura of power he exuded, perhaps. If she possessed a fraction of his assertiveness, she thought as she watched him drive out of the parking lot, she wouldn't be sitting here feeling so helpless and inept.

"As you can see, my father isn't too happy about what's been going on between Kim and me," Kyle said. "But he does seem concerned about her. He asks about her condition all the time. When I stopped by to see her last night, he was outside the ICU talking to Nurse Thomas."

Kyle grimaced. "After I look in on Kim, I suppose I'll have to go out to dinner with my in-laws and act like a 'happily married man.' I'm sick of pretending something I don't feel. It isn't fair to Marisa either."

As Susan entered the ICU late Monday afternoon for the second time that day, she noticed there was a patient, an elderly, gray-haired man in one of the other beds. Anne Thomas was hovering over him, checking his vital signs.

Susan looked down at the still form of her sister. Closing her eyes, she tried to see beyond the pale, bandaged face into the heart of Kim's being. Who was she? What was she really like? Susan had witnessed her deep depression, her bitterness, and vengeful rhetoric. But there was another side to Kim, a laughing, gregarious side. At least, there had been once.

Kim stirred slightly. Her eyes opened, narrow slits behind swollen lids.

As she peered up at her, Susan saw recognition in Kim's eyes.

"Welcome back," Susan said softly. "How do you feel?"

Kim groaned. "Like a Mack truck ran over me. Where am I?" She stared at the flowers on a stand alongside her. Susan suspected the large arrangement in a vase alongside the one she had brought were from Kyle.

"You're in the hospital," Susan told her sister.

"How did I get here?' Kim's voice was weak and filled with confusion. "What happened?"

"We'll talk about that later." Susan brushed a strand of long, pale hair back from the shoulder of her sister's hospital gown.

Squeezing her eyes tightly together, Kim's brow furrowed in deep concentration. "I remember now. Things really got screwed up...."

"Don't try to talk," Susan cautioned.

"I have to say this before it's too late."

Anne Thomas moved away from the patient in the other bed and came over to Kim's bedside. "You mustn't exert yourself," she warned as she placed her fingers on Kim's pulse.

"I have to talk to my sister." Kim reached out for Susan's hand. "I hope you'll find it in your heart to forgive me."

"This can wait," Susan said as Anne Thomas took hold of her arm and motioned toward the doorway.

Kim shook her head from side to side. Reaching out for Susan once again, she protested, "No! It can't wait. I have to tell you now, so you'll understand the way it was."

Apprehension chilling her to the bone, Susan pulled out of the stern-faced nurse's grasp, and moved back to Kim's bed.

In a faint, faltering voice, pausing occasionally to renew her strength, Kim explained how Al Preston had approached her after Brad's death. How, together, they had conspired to steal industrial secrets from Markum Manufacturing. She told how, after falling in love with Kyle, she had tried to back out of their deal, but Preston had threatened to expose her to Gil.

"I care about Kyle," Kim agonized. "I didn't mean for it to happen, but it did."

"You have to leave," Nurse Thomas insisted to Susan. "Your sister is too weak for this."

"No. Bug off," Kim said, anger momentarily strengthening her voice. "I need to speak to my sister. *Privately.*"

Lips narrowing, Anne Thomas unwillingly moved over to her desk.

In a voice barely audible at times, Kim told how she had planned to kill Preston if he didn't let her off the hook. How she fabricated the story of the break-in attempt to achieve credibility if it became necessary, that she thought she was being burglarized again and feared for her life.

"I didn't think charges would be brought against me if I were trying to protect my home and my virtue," Kim's voice faltered. She took a deep breath. "I was desperate. It was the only way I could see to get out of the mess I'd gotten myself into."

Susan couldn't believe what she was hearing. This devious, scheming woman was her sister, the sister she had always envied and wanted to be like? For an instant, Susan withdrew in horror. She wanted to flee from the room and Kim's presence as fast as she could.

"Preston was a low life." Kim spoke in an imploring voice as she clung to Susan's hand. "I knew he wouldn't leave me alone, that he'd keep insisting that I had to get something out of Kyle."

"So, when he came to see you, you..." Susan said in a voice filled with horror.

"He called me first," Kim interrupted. "When I told him I wanted out he threatened to tell Kyle how I was using him. I said I'd go to Kyle and tell him myself, that he would forgive me. It was a bluff. I wasn't *that* sure of Kyle." Kim's explanation was slow and riddled with pauses.

Mouth pulled into a tight line, Anne Thomas shoved back her chair in front of the desk and stood up. "That's enough. You have to leave now, Mrs. Edwards, or I'll call security. Your sister cannot tolerate anymore of this."

Susan patted Kim's hand "Maybe you should rest. We can talk later."

Kim shook her head. "No. I may not be around later. I almost told Kyle what was going on as he was leaving my place the morning you were there. But he was on his way down the driveway, and I couldn't stop him."

"I told Preston on the phone that I was through with him, but an hour later he was on my doorstep. He made me go over all the ways I'd tried to extract information about the security system from Kyle. I exaggerated to make it sound good. In order to get rid of Preston, I said I'd work on Kyle some more. I didn't really intend to..." Kim paused to catch her breath. "I just wanted out so he and I could be together. So I could start a new life."

Out of the corner of her eye, Susan saw Anne Thomas stalk out of the room, on her way to summon security, no doubt.

"So when Preston walked out of the house you shot him..."

"The Weasel—Preston is dead?" Kim's voice was hoarse in disbelief.

"He was shot on the walkway outside your house."

"I didn't shoot him," Kim denied weakly. "He went out of the house before I got the gun from the drawer. I went after him...I was afraid he was going to Kyle..." Kim's voice was raspy, her breathing ragged and labored. It was obvious she had little strength left, that she was holding on by sheer will power. Tears glistened in the corners of her bloodshot eyes, slid slowly down her swollen and discolored cheeks. "I'm sorry for making such a mess of things."

Susan saw that her sister was near collapse. Clinging to Kim's hand, Susan pleaded, "Are you sure you didn't shoot Preston and flee in your car?"

"No! No! I didn't shoot him...I didn't go anywhere in my car. I pointed the gun at him. I intended to threaten him, yes, even shoot him if he refused to leave me alone. I didn't get the chance...."

Kim's face contorted in a sudden spasm. The veins in her neck were prominent and throbbing as she struggled to sit up. The IV jiggled precariously.

"Are you satisfied?" Anne Thomas snapped as she re-entered the room, followed by a man in a blue uniform. "I warned you...."

Quickly, the nurse moved over to Kim and along with Susan and the security guard, held onto Kim and tried to calm her down.

There was a wildness in Kim's eyes as she lay back on the pillow. "Don't hit me again!" she pleaded harshly. "Don't hit me...."

"It's all right," Susan comforted as she held onto Kim's shoulder. "It's me...Susan. I won't let anyone hurt you."

By what Kim had said, it sounded as if, as Harry theorized, Preston had taken the gun away from Kim and beaten her with it. Yet the scar-faced man was dead, and the weapon that had undoubtedly been used to kill him had been found in the glove compartment of Kim's car.

Had she taken it away from Preston? Fear made Amazons of people. Or had the gun gone off in the scuffle? No, Preston had been shot in the back, as if he had been running away. Had Kim killed him, then blocked it out of her mind? It was possible her head injuries were affecting her. How much truth was there to anything Kim had uttered?

Susan leaned closer to her sister so she could hear better. "Did Preston beat you with the gun?"

Kim tossed her head from side to side in denial. "He didn't touch me. I don't know how…"

Susan leaned closer to her sister. "Who did this to you, Kim? Tell me!"

"It…it was…" Lapsing into silence, she lay motionless on the white, sterile sheets.

"I hope you're happy now," Nurse Thomas said angrily. "I should have made you leave. If your sister dies, you'll be the one who's responsible…."

There was no sound in the room except Kim's labored breathing. Her unconsciousness crushed Susan's hopes of learning who had beaten her sister or what had happened, for now. Then Susan was seized by a paralyzing fear. If Kim hadn't driven away in her car, as she claimed, how was it that her car had been found halfway down the embankment?

Someone else must have placed her in it and driven it away. Had it been intentionally driven off the cliff with Kim in it? If Kim hadn't shot Preston, who had and why? How had Preston gotten out to Kim's place? From what Kim had said, he had come into the house alone. Perhaps a second person whom she was unaware of had driven him out there and remained in the car. Susan's head was swimming with questions. It was all so confusing. Nothing made sense. If Kim had shot Preston, why hadn't the second person—if there had been one—reported it to the police?

Her head reeling dizzily, Susan stumbled backward, groping for the chair behind her. Waves of nausea rising in her throat, she dropped onto the chair. Bowing her head, she covered her ears with her hands and tried to stop the whirling, the confusion inside her head. It was all too horrible! Too much to comprehend!

The security guard took hold of her arm. "Let's go, Miss."

Susan struggled to her feet. "I'll be back," she promised the still form on the bed. As she stumbled out of the room, she prayed that, somehow, Kim had heard her and understood.

Susan knew she must find Reid and tell him what she had learned. If someone other than Preston had beaten Kim, and for some unfathomable reason, had driven her car off the cliff with her in it, now that she was alive and conscious and could identify him, that person might try again. He—or she couldn't have Kim reporting his part in whatever had happened. Security would have to be posted outside her hospital room to protect her.

The memory of the despair on Marisa's face when Kyle had left to be at Kim's bedside after she had been found was engraved in Susan's mind like letters chiseled in stone. Marisa was a desperate woman. Desperate enough, Susan was certain, to want Kim out of the picture. To make it happen.

Chapter 25

Elongated shadows stretched out from the trees and buildings as Susan hurried across the hospital's parking lot in the reddening light of the setting sun. Her mind was reeling from what Kim had told her. Her sister was near death's door. Someone could well be waiting to push her through it. Kim had denied killing Preston. If that were true, someone else had and Kim could identify them.

"Susan!" a deep voice called out.

Looking in the direction of the sound, Susan saw Gil Markum striding toward her, his footfall making thuds on the parking lots' hard surface. His thick, dark brows were drawn together in a deep frown.

He halted in front of her. "Where are you going in such a rush?"

"I'm on my way to find Reid Elison. If you're looking for Kyle, he's not with Kim."

"I'm not looking for Kyle. Marisa's father had a heart attack last night shortly after we had dinner together. He's in ICU. I thought I'd stop by and see how he's doing."

"He must be the new patient that's in with Kim."

Gil's sharp eyes were alert. "Has your sister regained consciousness?"

"She was awake for a few minutes."

"Did she tell you what happened to her?" There was an apprehension in Gil's expression, a deep curiosity that revealed his concern.

The less said the better, Susan determined, even to Gil. "She started to before she collapsed, but...." Susan gestured helplessly.

"Then why are you in such a hurry to find Elison?" Gil wanted to know.

"Because.... to insure Kim's safety."

"To insure her safety? Who do you think is going to harm her in the hospital? Why would they want to?"

"I don't believe what happened to Kim was an accident. I think someone tried to kill her and bungled the job. She will identify that person when she regains consciousness." *If* she regained consciousness. "I think he—or she—will come back and try to make sure that doesn't happen."

Gil gave Susan a condescending smile. "I agree what's happened to your sister is a terrible thing, but someone wants her dead? You're letting your imagination run away with you."

"Don't I wish, but I don't believe that I am."

Gil ran his large fingers through his thick shock of white hair, as if he were embarrassed. "I have a favor to ask. I have some business to take care of, but my car is acting up and I don't think I should drive it. Could I get you to give me a ride home? I'll call the garage from there and have the Lincoln towed in to be checked."

A wave of pleasure flooded over Susan, warming her blood and bringing a smile to her lips. From his actions, his animosity toward her had faded. "Your new car is giving you trouble?" Her brows arched teasingly.

Gil gave her a sheepish smile. "No cracks, please. I don't think it's anything major, but I don't want to drive it if I don't have to." He was his old charming self again. Smiling into her eyes, mesmerizing her with his essence. Her heart soared as he placed his hand on her arm.

"I thought you were on your way into the hospital to see Marisa's father," Susan said.

"I can come back later in my Blazer. I called Kyle to come and get me, but no one was home. Since you're here, Susan, I'll take advantage of you. I hope you don't mind." His hand tightening on her arm, he peered down at her, a mocking smile curling his lips.

As their eyes met, Susan could feel her bones melting and her pulse pounding in her throat. "Of course I don't mind." then she sobered. "But first I want to talk to Reid and have a guard placed outside Kim's hospital room."

"I still think you're being overly imaginative," Gil said with a little laugh. "I doubt if you'll be able to get a hold of Elison. I saw him driving down the street a few minutes ago."

Dismay washed over Susan. "I have to talk to someone."

"Look, there's a phone booth in the corner of the parking lot," Gil said. "The sheriff is a good friend of mine. Stop by the booth, and I'll give him a call and have him put a guard outside Kim's door for you."

Susan gave Gil a grateful smile. "Thanks, but I better take care of this myself, just to make sure it's done."

Gil took her arm. "That's your Skyhawk, isn't it?" he asked, steering her toward her car. "I assure you everything will be taken care of. I'll talk to Sheriff Larson personally. After you take me home, you can come back here and check to make sure everything's all right."

Susan conceded that the results would undoubtedly be quicker and more certain if Gil took care of the matter. He was an influential man. People jumped at his command, without a doubt vied with each other to please him. She would find Reid later and talk to him. The important thing was to get a guard at Kim's door.

Gil looked out of place as he sat in the passenger's seat, Susan thought as she slid behind the steering wheel. She doubted if he allowed someone else to be in the driver's seat on many occasions. As she switched on the ignition and placed the car in gear, Gil removed a pair of sunglasses from his shirt pocket and slipped them on.

When they reached the phone booth, Susan pulled to a halt. As Gil stood in the small cubicle, she saw him dig into his pants pocket for some coins and insert them in the slot. She saw him dial the numbers, the movement of his lips as he talked into the receiver. Minutes later, his burly frame was seated next to her again.

"That's taken care of," he said. "No need to worry anymore."

She gave him a small smile as she shifted into 'Drive' again. "I don't know how to thank you."

"No thanks are necessary. I'm happy to help you in any way I can."

In spite of his assurance that there was no need to worry anymore, Susan's fears and concern for her sister hadn't diminished. They wouldn't disappear, she knew, until Kim regained consciousness and whoever had tried to kill her was found and put away.

"Go down Randolph and turn onto Lakeview," Gil directed as she drove toward the hospital's exit.

She cast him a quick glance. "Those are back streets. Wouldn't it be better if I took Center Avenue to Willow?"

"There's less traffic on Randolph and Lakeview."

It would take at least forty-five minutes to take Gil home and return to Lake Center, Susan determined as she followed his directions. She tried to ease her mind by telling herself that, by this time, the sheriff had probably ordered a guard to be placed outside Kim's hospital room.

As Susan neared the next intersection, Gil's deep, grating voice interrupted her thoughts. "Take West Ridge Wood Road," he instructed. When Susan shot him another puzzled glance, he said, "It's shorter to my place if you go that way, and since you're in a hurry...."

"West Ridge Wood is also winding and treacherous," Susan pointed out. "I won't be able to drive very fast."

Recalling it from her childhood, she knew the road he had instructed her to take led around Long Lake and came out on the southeast side, near Kim's driveway, where it joined the highway east of Lake Center. The terrain on the north and west of the lake was hilly and densely wooded.

Gil grinned at her. "What's your hurry?" Sobering, he said, "There's hardly any traffic on it at this time of the evening. You'll make better time even if it's a little rolly and curving."

Susan was dubious, but not wanting to appear ungrateful, she did as she had been directed. Gil had been kind enough to call the sheriff's department and make arrangements for a guard to be placed at Kim's hospital door. The least she could do, Susan conceded, was to follow his instructions.

When they were five or six miles out on the gravel road, Gil pointed to a spot ahead. "Pull over. There's a beautiful view of the sunset at this time of the evening."

Susan's heart warmed at the thought that he wanted to share the moment with her. But how could she enjoy the sunset when Kim's life was hanging by a thread, when Kim might never see another sunset? "I don't know if I should take the time...."

"Stop worrying," Gil chided. "I took care of things, didn't I? We won't stay long. After all, I may never see you again."

"Of course you will," Susan quickly assured him. "I'll come back from time to time to visit Kim and Harry." If she and Mark got back together and she moved California, she realized those visits might be few and far between.

"But there may never be a sunset like this one," Gil stressed, smiling at her.

The warmth of his smile heated her blood and sent ripples down to her toes. Letting up on the accelerator, she pulled over to the side of the road. They were on a hill overlooking the lake. The embankment plunged downward for three hundred feet or more. In the distance, the lake was bathed in pinkish-gray twilight. A flock of loons flew over the lake, their plaintive cries sounding in the still evening air.

"Pull off the road a little farther," Gil urged. "We can see better."

Shifting into 'Drive', Susan eased ahead several yards, then shifted back into 'Park' and engaged the emergency brake. "That's far enough. I don't want to drive over the side of the cliff like..." The spot where

Kim had been found was similar to this one and not far from here, according to what Reid had told her. As the thought of what had happened to Kim came into her mind, goosebumps erupted all over Susan's body.

"Is something wrong?" Gil asked. "Are you afraid of heights?"

"I was thinking about what happened to Kim."

"It was a terrible accident. She must have been driving too fast."

"I think it was meant to *look* like an accident. And I don't think she killed Preston."

A deep frown furrowing his wide brow, Gil fixed his eyes on Susan. "Why do you think that? Was it something your sister said? I thought she didn't tell you anything."

"She didn't, but she was about to. As soon as she regains consciousness she'll tell us who killed Preston and tried to kill her. Then that monster, whoever he is, will get what he deserves."

"*If* she regains consciousness again," Gil emphasized.

"Of course she will." Susan was adamant, as if by thinking positively, she could make it happen.

"I wouldn't bet on it." There was finality in Gil's tone.

Chapter 26

Deciding to check and see if Kim Hastings' condition had improved by now so he could talk to her, Reid pulled his patrol car into a space between two cars in the hospital's parking lot. He turned off the ignition and was about to remove the key when he saw Gil Markum climb out of his white Lincoln and stride toward the entrance.

The big man must be visiting someone, Reid thought. Considering that Kyle had been having an affair with Kim, it was doubtful the older Markum would be going to visit her.

Then Reid's attention turned to a slender figure dressed in shorts and a bare-midriff top coming out of the hospital and starting across the parking lot. It was Susan, he saw. She and Gil stopped and talked to each other several minutes. Then Gil took her arm and together, they walked to her car and got in. Reid scowled. If they were going somewhere together, why wasn't Gil driving his Lincoln?

Reid sensed the two of them weren't exactly strangers. Susan had been defensive of Gil when they had gone out to his place. It had been evident she was glad he could account for his whereabouts the time Preston was killed.

She didn't know what kind of man she was dealing with, Reid thought with a scowl. But power and wealth were cogent aphrodisiacs, qualities a lot of people often found hard to resist.

Reid's gaze followed Susan's car as she drove toward the exit, as she stopped by the phone booth and Gil made a call. He watched as she drove out of the parking lot and merged with the traffic on the street.

Shoving his fingers through his thick, dark hair, Reid scratched his head. What business could the two of them possibly have together? Did it have something to do with Kim or Al Preston? The thought that it might be personal, possibly of an intimate nature, left a bad taste in his mouth.

Switching on the ignition, Reid backed the patrol car out of the parking space and made for the exit. Just before he reached it, the signal light at the intersection changed and, because of the heavy traffic, he couldn't make a left turn onto the street. Young people were cruising main, their car stereos blaring. And there were the moviegoers and the usual sightseers. Young males whose testosterone was in overdrive. Reid swore under his breath. Straining his eyes, he peered down the street, trying to pick out Susan's blue Skyhawk in the line of traffic. It was nowhere in sight.

Switching on the patrol car's siren and flashing lights, he swung out onto the sidewalk, and drove to the end of the line of traffic. Then he swung out onto the street. Tires screeched as the oncoming traffic braked to keep from hitting the patrol car. Anger was apparent on the faces of the drivers. Reid could see their lips moving, could decipher the profanity directed at him.

In the street now, he turned off the flashers and the siren so Susan and Gil wouldn't know he was tailing them. Weaving in and out of the traffic, Reid sped in the direction they had driven. His eyes searched the line of vehicles in front of him for the Skyhawk.

It had vanished from sight.

As he raced by the side streets, he cast a quick glance down them in case Susan had turned off the main street.

He saw nothing.

Where the hell could they have gone?

When he reached the city limits, the traffic had thinned and there were only three or four cars in front of him. None of them was a blue Skyhawk.

"Damn!" he exclaimed, striking the steering wheel with a clenched fist. He'd lost them!

Chapter 27

Tensing at the decisiveness in Gil's words, Susan's head jerked around. She stared at him, her eyes wide and a sinking sensation in the pit of her stomach. "What do you mean it's not going to happen? Of course it is."

Gil removed his sunglasses and slid them in his shirt pocket. "Not if I can help it," he said again.

Dear God! Susan gasped, the skin prickling on the back of her neck. The look in Gil's eyes seemed to slice through her before he hooded them.

"It was you!" Her voice was a harsh whisper. "You did that to Kim! You tried to kill my sister!" Everything froze—a photograph suspended and enlarged within Susan's mind, shone with a multi-faceted light. Once again she saw Gil's ashen face when she told Kyle that Kim had been found. She recalled Marisa's statement that she had seen Al Preston at Gil's place, his concern and questions about Kim's condition.

The significance of Gil's words was almost incomprehensible to Susan, but it was all there in his chilling blue eyes.

Her stomach muscles quivered. Had he hated Kim enough to want her dead because she was having an affair with his son? Had he found out she was using Kyle to try to steal corporate secrets from his firm?

Was that the reason for his strange behavior at the Country Club when he discovered she was Kim's sister?

Gil's voice sounded in her ear. "I'm sorry it has to be this way, but things have gone too far to turn back now. It's you or me, and it's not gonna be me."

Fear seized Susan, draining the blood from her veins and sapping her strength. "You didn't call the sheriff, did you? You only pretended to." She edged away from him.

"I called my home number and spoke into the answering service," Gil said. "Sorry. I have no choice."

Susan's stomach lurched. He was going to kill her the same way he had tried to kill Kim. This time he would make certain his intended victim didn't survive. Men like Gil didn't get where they were by making mistakes.

There hadn't been another car on the winding dirt road since she had turned onto it. That was the reason Gil suggested they take it, Susan saw now. There was less chance that anyone would see them together. She was certain there had been nothing wrong with his car. It had been a way to get her out here alone. He had beaten Kim, placed her in her car and let it roll over the cliff. He was about to repeat his grisly deed.

Gil's rugged countenance was hard and chiseled, like glacial ice. "Nobody uses my son or tries to screw me over and gets away with it. Nobody! When I've taken care of you, I'm going back and finish the job on your conniving sister. I thought she was dead when I put the car in gear and headed it off the cliff."

Susan felt the heat of his anger. As the enormity of the situation she was in swept over her, Susan was glad she was the one Gil was holding hostage. Kim, lying helpless and near death with only one nurse on duty at night in the Intensive Care Unit, would be easy prey. Gil would ask to see Marisa's father and be granted permission. He could easily step between the curtains that separated the beds, move over to Kim's bed unnoticed, and disconnect the tubes that were her lifeline.

Perhaps that's what he'd come to do when they had met in the parking lot. It wouldn't be that difficult; he would be in the ICU, visiting Marisa's father—or so he said. No one would know what had happened. As long as everything was quiet, the nurse probably wouldn't check on Kim for some time. If, by chance, she did check and suspected foul play, she wouldn't suspect one of Lake Center's most upstanding citizens. More likely, she would blame it on the inefficiency or neglect of someone on the hospital staff.

And even if she suspected Gil, she wouldn't be able to prove it, or stand up against the battery of lawyers he would hire to defend himself if need be. The attorneys would make it appear as if the tubes had come disconnected accidentally, make it look as if the nurse had been derelict. Good lawyers could make black appear to be white, and the affluent Gil could afford lots of good lawyers.

She couldn't give up yet, Susan told herself, even though she, like Kim, was balancing on the edge of death. She must stall for time, stretch every remaining moment as far as she could. Maybe, just maybe, around the corner, help was approaching in the form of a chance motorist.

"How did you find out what Kim was doing?" Susan asked.

In a calm, grating voice, as if he were giving a business report, Gil explained. "Preston *was* at the house. He told me what he and Kim had been planning, how he was being double-crossed and wanted to get even. For a price and the promise that I'd let him off, he told me he'd give me the name of his partner and all the proof I wanted. All I had to do was take him out to his partner's place and listen outside an open window while he drew her out enough to confirm her part in it."

Gil's lips twisted into an ugly smile. "Imagine my surprise when I discovered his partner was none other than your sister, the sneaky little bitch who was having an affair with my son. She didn't give a damn about Kyle. She was using him to get to me."

Susan could smell the venom on Gil's breath.

"Your sister bragged how she had Kyle wrapped around her finger," Gil went on. "I heard everything outside her living room window. When Preston came out of the house, she was behind him with a gun. She didn't know I had come there with him. I parked my Blazer partway up her driveway, and hid it in the bushes. He had walked up ahead of me to talk to her. When I came round the corner of the house, I startled her. She turned the gun on me, but I yanked it out of her hand. She fought like a hellcat, clawing at my face and arms, tore my shirt."

Susan glanced at the red welts on his arm. "So that's how you got those scratches."

Gil grunted. "She's got claws like a damned tom cat. I had to whack her alongside the head with the gun a couple of times to get her off me. She fell to the ground."

Susan had all she could do to keep from scratching out Gil's eyes. But she waited for the rest of his story, praying, always praying that help was just around the corner. But that possibility was fleeting with each passing minute. She had noticed that there were no residences or lake cabins along this particular section of the road. Under ordinary circumstances, the road was lightly traveled. Tonight, seemingly, not at all.

"I thought Kim was dead," Gil continued. "I could tell that Preston thought so, too. I knew he had me, that he'd blackmail me for the rest of my life. I could already see the dollar signs in his beady eyes. I told him he was in it as deep as I was, and if he tried anything, I'd say he killed her. Who would take his word over mine? We got into a big argument. The chicken shit took off running, and I shot him. I had to."

"I put your sister's unconscious body in her car to make it look like your sister had killed him and ran off. I wiped my prints off the gun and put it, along with Preston's wallet to implicate her even more, into the glove compartment of her car. Then I drove the car up the road to where the embankment was the steepest and got out. I shoved the car in 'Drive' and let it roll over the cliff."

Gil's fists clenched and unclenched in reflection. "If she wasn't dead from the beating, falling that far into a pile of boulders would have killed her. It was my lousy luck the damn car got hung up halfway down."

Overcome with horror, Susan drew back, away from him. "And then you walked back to Kim's house and your Blazer and went home...."

"I kept to the woods so no one would see me if they came along," Gil said. "I was a little late meeting your uncle at the Country Club for the interview because I had to shower and change clothes."

His explanation of the heinous crime he had committed had taken no more than two or three minutes. Susan knew her time was running out. She was horrified at the extent of the big man's barbaric behavior. After pistol-whipping Kim into unconsciousness and sending her car off an embankment, after shooting a man in cold blood, he had appeared at the Country Club to be interviewed by one of his victim's foster father as one of the area's most prominent citizens. Anger bubbled and simmered through Susan's blood stream. She clenched her hands together to keep from reaching out and fastening them around his neck. What kind of man was he? How could she have been attracted to such a ruthless animal?

"When Marisa told me your sister was playing around with Kyle, I wanted to wring her lousy neck," Gil went on, his voice seething with anger. "I walked over to her place one night, following the beach around the lake from my place to hers. I wanted her out of my son's life. I don't know what I intended to do. Threaten her, scare the hell out of her, I guess. Then I saw her, at least I thought it was her, walking along the beach. I saw red at the sight of her strolling along as if she didn't have a care in the world. If she were found drowned, no one would think anything of it. She'd simply gone for a swim and suffered a cramp."

Susan gasped. "It was you on the beach that night! You were the one who tried to drown me!"

"It was hard to see in the darkness, but when the scarf slid off your head, I saw your short hair and knew you weren't Kim. Imagine my surprise when I learned from Harry at the Country Club that you were her sister. I put two and two together and realized it was you that I had tried to drown." He draped his arm over the backrest behind her.

Susan's shoulder pressed against the car door as she tried to lean farther away from him. "I wasn't wearing a swim suit that night on the beach. The police would have been smart enough to know it was highly unlikely that anyone would go swimming with their clothes on."

"Why not?" Gil challenged. "It was a hot night and you were alone. You wanted to go for a quick dip to cool off. But that doesn't matter now."

Susan's heart plummeted. "You can't get away with murder no matter who you are."

"I won't be found out if the two people who know what's happened—you and your sister—aren't alive to tell anyone. Believe me, I'll be more professional about it than those two clowns who tried to bankrupt my company. A couple of damn amateurs with shit for brains."

Her head spinning, Susan grasped for something, *anything*, to keep alive. "I...I thought you and I were friends, that I meant something to you..."

"I told you I had a strange feeling I'd met you before, and I couldn't let go of that feeling. Now I know it was because of that night on the beach. Because you look like your sister. If the two of you remain alive, I'll be ruined. I can't let that happen."

Susan's hands were shaking. Her heart was hammering so hard it was threatening to jump out of her chest. "I won't tell anyone what you did. And Kim may never regain consciousness. Even if she does, she won't say anything either. After all, she intended to kill Preston herself."

"She's out to get me. She won't keep her mouth shut about my beating her up. She'll know it was me who shot Preston. It's me she wanted, not him. He was just an accomplice in her little scheme."

"In exchange for her life and mine, she'll say she killed Preston in self defense," Susan reasoned in desperation. "I'll talk her into it." She was fully aware she was no match for Gil's brute strength. But her life and Kim's was at stake. She would do anything, promise anything in order to survive.

Gil's mouth twisted into a cold smile. "Nice try, but no dice. You know as well as I do as soon as you're out of my reach, you'll run for the sheriff's office. It's really too bad you had to get involved in this. I find your naiveté quite charming."

For an instant, there was a softening on his square-jawed countenance. Then his face was like stone again, his eyes hard and unyielding. He reached to turn on the ignition. "But you are involved, aren't you, and you're going to have to be dealt with."

Like a glitch in a business deal, Susan thought. She would be crushed and tossed aside like an error-ridden business report.

"I lied to you," Susan said in one last desperate effort. "Kim did say something when she was conscious. Nurse Thomas was a witness. If anything happens to me she'll go to the police."

"Nurse Thomas?" Gil laughed coldly. "I don't think so. It's amazing what we'll say or do to save our neck, isn't it? I'm sure you can see my position, that's what I'm doing too, can't you?"

"It could work out for both of us," Susan stressed. "You don't have to…"

"Kim didn't tell you who beat her up, and Nurse Thomas won't go to the authorities. I paid her to get everyone out of the room, including you, if your sister regained consciousness and started talking. I emphasized that Kim was special to me and if she exerted herself and had a relapse, I would hold her nurse personally responsible. That I'd have her job."

"You wasted your time and your money," Susan said. "Kim did talk to me. Oh, your friend Anne Thomas tried to get me out of the room, but I refused to leave." Susan knew she was on the brink of losing her life, less than a minute and a few feet away. Yet she couldn't give up without a fight. Concession would be fatal. She would grab onto him wherever she could. Nothing short of death itself would force her to relinquish her hold.

Gil gave her a mocking smile. "Nice try," he said again.

Fingers spread and curved like talons, she lunged for his face. She would scratch out his eyes. Tear his cold, handsome face to shreds. She would hold onto his shirt, his arms, anything, and would not let go. Never, as long as there was a breath of life left in her body.

She felt her nails tearing into his flesh, saw the livid red streaks on his cheek. Her lips curved into an icy smile at the pleasure of it. He had reduced her to something less than human. She had changed from a spineless, babbling idiot into an animal possessed by a primitive rage that blurred her vision and filled her with an uncontrollable urge to kill.

Then his hands were around her wrists like steel bands, rendering her helpless. His mouth was a grim line, his cold eyes shining like polished steel. Under the strain, the muscles in his massive neck popped out. One huge hand moved to cover her face and her nose, to cut off her breathing. He was going to smother her. Strangling would leave telltale marks on her throat. When she was discovered, *if* she were discovered, a bundle of broken bones at the bottom of the cliff, no one would check her lungs. The cause of death would be obvious. If her car were to catch fire, to explode and burn upon impact, there would be nothing left except a black charred mass, twisted steel, and blistered and blackened paint. It had happened that way with Brad.

Susan tried to open her mouth, to gasp for air, but Gil's hand was clamped tightly across her face. Her lungs felt as if they were about to burst. Her eyes felt as if they were about to pop out of their sockets.

As she struggled, kicking and kneeing him, Gil's hand slipped to the side of her mouth. She bit down viciously. With a yelp of pain, he thrust her away from him. She saw his arm come up, felt his fist smash into her face. She fell back against the car door, pain shooting through her head and blood spurting from her nose.

Through the wave of blackness that washed over her, she saw him reach for the ignition again. She heard the motor catch and hum. He was going to leap out, leaving her and the Skyhawk to plunge downward into oblivion. His attention diverted momentarily, Gil didn't see her reach for the door handle, press down on it. The door swung open. She tumbled out, losing one of her sandals. Picking herself up, she took off stumbling, running down the road.

Slowing down a bit, using the back of her hand, she wiped at the blood that trickled from her nose. Shooting a hasty look over her shoulder, she saw that Gil was moving her car back onto the road.

Lake Center was miles away—at least four or five miles. More than she could run.

She saw the car coming toward her, Gil hunched over the steering wheel.

Turning her attention to the road ahead again, Susan increased her speed. Her face pounded with every step she took. Gravel cut into the bottom of her sandalless foot like shards of crushed glass. Her body was damp with perspiration. Another quick glance over her shoulder revealed that Gil was gaining on her. She could almost feel the car striking her, smashing her bones, crushing her under its tires. But there was nothing to do except keep running. Running.

The breath tore at her throat. The rapid hammering of her heart was like a knife stabbing into her chest. She scarcely had enough strength left to place one foot in front of the other, yet she knew she must.

Her life depended on it; Kim's life depended on it.

Gil, too, was fighting for his life, to keep from going to prison for murder. Another homicide would make little difference. He couldn't be executed twice.

It was survival of the most desperate, the most determined.

CHAPTER 28

Susan knew if she remained on the road she would be overtaken and run down within minutes. The woods, she realized, wouldn't provide her with refuge for long. Gil could easily outrun her on foot. He would swoop down on her like a hawk on a hapless sparrow. Yet the dense growth of trees would provide her with protection from being crushed under the wheels of her own automobile.

She turned into the ditch, stumbling as she did so, losing her other sandal. Recovering her balance, she glanced back and saw the Skyhawk bearing down on her. Gil braked to a screeching halt, sending particles of gravel spraying out behind it. The car door swung open and he leapt out.

Please, God, help me! Susan prayed. It wasn't only her own life that was in danger, but Kim's, too.

Then the sound of a siren blaring cut into the twilight. Susan saw a whirling yellow light in the distance. Seconds later, a squad car slid to a grinding halt alongside the Skyhawk. Reid jumped out.

"What's going on here?" he yelled.

Gil froze—an arm's length away from Susan. Turning around carefully, he stepped back onto the road a short distance from Reid. "Everything's cool. Just a little disagreement."

Reid looked at Susan. "Is that what's going on?"

"He's trying to kill me," she panted, her breath tearing at her throat. Disbelief shone on Reid's face. "Is that true, Markum?"

"It's ridiculous," Gil denied. "Susan's just overwrought."

"He killed Preston and tried to kill Kim," Susan charged. "He's trying to kill me to keep me from telling what he did."

Reid reached for his gun. "Is that the way it is, Markum?"

"Put that thing away," Gil urged quietly.

"I think you and I should go down to the station and have a little talk." Reid pointed the gun at Gil. "Get this straightened out."

As Reid was speaking, Gil began to edge toward the deputy.

"Stay where you are," Reid ordered.

"Okay. Okay." Gil held up his hands in a gesture of concession.

Suddenly, unexpectedly, he lurched forward. With a quick, wide swing of his arm, he knocked the gun out of Reid's grasp. The weapon flew into the air, then fell to the ground, its momentum sending it sliding under the front of the patrol car.

Recovering from his surprise, Reid clenched his fists together and swung out, striking Gil on the jaw. The large man staggered back, reaching out to the patrol car for support. Like a flash, he was in control again, his huge fists swinging furiously. Reid dodged several blows. The next one struck him, staggering him. Then his fist smashed into Gil's face again. The white-haired man stumbled backward.

"Give it up, Markum!" Reid commanded. "You're under arrest for resisting an officer, and if what Susan's says is true, for kidnapping and murder, too."

Gil grimaced as he rubbed his hand across his jaw. "No one's arresting me."

Dropping his hand, he charged at Reid like a blind bull. He grabbed onto Reid, began to struggle with him. Susan watched helplessly as the two men staggered back and forth, fists flying, grunting and cursing under their breath.

The gun! Susan despaired. She had to get the gun. Getting down on her stomach, she reached out and groped under the squad car. At first, she felt nothing. And then there was the touch of cold steel on her fingertips. Clasping her fingers around the gun, she inched backward. Gravel dug into the soft flesh of her arms and elbows, her bare legs, but she scarcely noticed.

Gun in hand, she got to her feet.

The two men were fighting in the ditch along the roadside now. Suddenly, Reid's foot slipped in the grass. Seizing the advantage, Gil's arm moved back. His fist shot out.

Susan heard bone smashing against bone, saw Reid stagger and go down. Lay still.

When Gil turned to her, she pointed the gun at him. "Stay where you are or I'll shoot!"

Ignoring the command, Gil slowly, deliberately moved toward her, a smile of triumph on his lips. His eyes were icy, his face bruised and bloodied.

I can't do this! Susan despaired. She had never shot a gun before. Yet she knew if she didn't do something, Gil would kill her and Reid. Kim, lying helpless in the hospital, would be next. The decision was hers to make, Susan realized. *Now!* No vacillating! No procrastinating!

Kill or be killed.

Barefooted, legs wide apart to steady their shaking, she lifted the gun and pointed it at Gil. "I said stop!"

He kept coming.

"Stop!" Susan ordered again. When Gil continued to advance toward her, she closed her eyes. The gun shaking unsteadily in her grip, and the odor of her fear stinging her nostrils, she squeezed the trigger.

The blast from the gun ripped through the stillness of the evening, deafening her, and reverberating through the woods. Opening her eyes, she saw dust and particles of gravel splattered onto Gil's shoes. He halted, a twisted smile curling his mouth.

"Stay right where you are or I'll pull the trigger again," Susan warned. "I won't miss this time."

Gil's thin lips twisted into a cold smile. "You won't shoot me. You haven't got the guts." He lunged at her.

Susan's finger tightened. Pulled.

Gil lurched forward, an expression of surprise on his face. "Why you bitch!" he growled. He stared at the trickle of blood trailing down the side of his arm where the bullet had grazed it.

Then he came toward her again. Slowly. Eyes red with rage.

Susan stood motionless, as if she were mesmerized by the sight. When he was almost upon her, she pulled the trigger again. The click of the trigger was louder than the sound of the gun firing had been minutes ago.

The gun had misfired or was out of bullets. She was unaware of how many shells the chamber held or if Reid had fired it before.

She squeezed the trigger again. Still nothing.

Gil was just a few feet away from her now. Drawing back her arm, she flung the gun at him with all her might.

The gun struck him in the forehead. His eyes widened in astonishment, then rolled upward, the whites widening. He stumbled, reached out for the fender of the squad car to keep from falling to the ground.

Out of the corner of her eye, Susan saw Reid stirring slightly. He would be of little help to her or himself in his dazed condition. Gil could easily outman him. If she could draw Gil away, hopefully Reid could recover his senses and call for backup.

Gil held onto the fender, shaking his head to clear it. Then he lurched toward her, staggering slightly.

Cutting across the road at an angle, Susan fled for the protection of the strip of woods separating the road from the lake. Thick, leafy underbrush closed around her, slapped her in the face and against her bare, shorts-clad legs as she plunged through the maze of trees, not stopping, not thinking, running for her life. Would this terrorizing never end!

She had to hurry. She had to find a way to think clearly, to outsmart this maniac, and save herself and Reid. If Gil caught her, he wouldn't let either one of them live. *Couldn't* let them live.

Pausing momentarily, her breathing labored, she heard the brush snapping and cracking.

He was behind her!

Even though it was unlikely he could see her any better than she could see him, she knew she gave her position away with every move she made.

Adrenaline surging through her, she ran faster than she thought she was capable of doing. Struggling to maintain her footing, she plowed through the tangled undergrowth and jumped over exposed roots, her bare feet bruised and bleeding. She put out a hand and managed to catch hold of trailing branches, used them to haul herself forward.

She paused momentarily to listen again. Over the rustle and sighs of the trees, she heard the brush snapping and crackling. He was not hurrying, but was still in relentless pursuit. He was, undoubtedly, confident that he would overtake her when she tired. And that would be any minute.

The road was off to her left, she knew, not that it would help her since there was no traffic on it. She had to stay hidden as much as possible. Until Gil gave up. Yet she knew he wouldn't do that. Couldn't do that. She was too much of a threat to him. He had to keep her from telling the authorities what she knew.

Yards in front of her she saw what looked like a clearing. Maybe there was a residence, help for her here.

She moved forward, then halted abruptly, her knees weakened in dismay.

She was near the edge of a steep cliff that fell down to the lake. Breathing painfully, her heart pounding, she stared at the rocks jutting out of the side of the cliff and scattered along the lakeshore below. A jump or fall would kill, at least cripple her.

Backing away from the ledge, she started running parallel to the cliff.

She stumbled ahead, breathless, fighting panic and fear, squinting against the brush as it slapped in her face and tore at her clothing. Her left eye had started to swell where Gil had struck her. She could barely see out of it.

She didn't notice Gil until she almost collided into him. He stood directly in front of her, eyes narrowed, shoulders heaving with exertion.

She stopped abruptly, gulping for air, hauled it in deep drafts. Within minutes she wouldn't be breathing if Gil had his way.

He moved toward her.

Susan cast a quick glance to the side, took several steps backward.

Quickly, he was upon her, fastening his hands around her throat. She struck at him blindly. Her blows bounced off his broad chest like ping-pong balls off taut netting.

Then she felt Gil stiffen and saw Reid burst out of the brush.

With a cry that came from deep within his throat, he launched himself at Gil, knocking him aside. As the two men began to fight, what Reid lacked in brute strength, he compensated for with skill and finesse, punching Gil repeatedly on his injured arm.

The big man grunted with pain. Returning the favor, he lowered his head and barreled into Reid's rib cage. He was like a blind bull. Unstoppable!

The blow sent Reid to his knees, groaning in agony.

"You bastard!" Susan shouted at the sound of Reid's tormented cry. She flung herself at Gil, shoving him off balance.

Recovering quickly, he grabbed her by the shoulder, and rammed her into a tree. She slumped against its base, her head spinning.

Through the stars flashing in her head, she saw Reid enter the fray again. Go at Gil with a vengeance.

They broke apart. Circled each other. Reid's gaze held the other man's, announcing that this would be a fight to the finish. Either he or

Gil would die. There was no room for compromise. With his superior strength and size, in spite of his injured arm, Susan feared Gil had the advantage. Desperation was a great ally, made men invincible. Reid could lose. And if he did, Gil would kill her, too.

Gil lunged for Reid. Reid stepped back. They were dangerously close to the cliff's edge. One wrong move and both of them would fall to a certain death.

And then it happened.

Gil's huge hand reached out, caught Reid's arm as the heel of Reid's shoe caught on something and he fought for his balance. They struggled for a moment, moving closer and closer toward the yawning precipice. Apparently realizing where they were, Gil released his hold on Reid and threw up his arms. But it was too late. Both men teetered there for a moment, then went over the edge.

Susan's horrified scream pierced the evening air.

Chapter 29

The Rescue Squad was working feverishly. Several emergency technicians were being lowered carefully down the side of the cliff.

As she stared down at the men, her bare feet so badly cut and bruised she could barely stand, Susan feared that no one could have survived the fall. Gil had struck a large rock on the lakeshore and his body lay there, limp and broken. Reid—her heart caught as she glanced over the edge—lay draped over an outcropping of small trees halfway down the cliff.

After she had seen them plunge over the cliff, she had hurried back to the patrol car and called for help.

"Do you think he's still alive?" she asked the deputy who had accompanied the Rescue Squad to the scene. Her voice was cracked and although he had urged her to move away from the edge of the cliff, she had refused. As if she stood there, praying for his survival, Reid wouldn't be dead.

The deputy shrugged. "He's had quite a fall. What happened here?"

The deputy and two members of the rescue squad stood beside her, peering over the cliff while two other men, ropes attached to their waist, made their way down to Reid. Nearby an ambulance and two medical technicians waited.

Without going into the details, Susan briefly explained about Gil's efforts to strangle her and the fight between Reid and Gil.

As she glanced over the cliff again, she saw that the men had reached Reid's side. A flurry of activity followed, with ropes and stretchers being assembled and instructions shouted to the members of the rescue squad waiting above.

Susan kept her gaze trained on Reid as he was pulled upward. The task seemed to take hours; in actuality it was less than twenty minutes.

"He's alive," a paramedic said after he had examined Reid.

As if on cue, Reid moaned.

Susan's head began to spin and her knees buckle with relief. She reached out for the deputy beside her. She'd heard him referred to as 'Johnson,' and remembered him as one of the lawmen at Kim's place when Al Preston's body was found.

Recovering her composure, she watched as, sweating and their faces red with exertion, the men hoisted the stretcher with Reid's still form on it into the waiting ambulance.

"Looks like you could use some treatment, too," Deputy Johnson said.

Susan cast a quick glance down the cliff where one of the men from the Rescue Squad was standing beside Gil's body, and talking on a cordless phone to one of the medics beside her.

"He's dead," the man announced, then closed and pocketed his phone.

Susan climbed into the back of the ambulance with Reid and the medical team. Another ambulance would bring Gil's body back later, after it was brought up from the lake shore, she was told.

As she peered at Reid, she knew it was a miracle he wasn't dead, too. If his fall hadn't been halted by the growth of trees on the side of the cliff—she didn't want to think about it.

She prayed as the paramedic worked over Reid. When another moan escaped from his lips, she reached out and took his hand in hers. Holding onto it, willing her strength into him, she closed her eyes and repeated her prayers over and over as the ambulance sped toward the hospital, its siren wailing in the late evening air.

The next few hours were a blur in Susan's mind. Reid was taken to the emergency room where it was discovered that, besides bruises and a possible concussion, several of his ribs were broken. He would undergo tests in the morning to see if he had internal injuries.

After having her own injuries treated, she returned to Reid's bedside in the intensive care unit. On the opposite end of the room, her sister still lay in a coma, the victim of the same man who was responsible for Reid's condition.

Susan's eye was blackening where Gil had struck her. There were cuts and bruises on her face and knees. Red welts crisscrossed her arms and legs. Her feet were so cut and bloodied she could scarcely hobble around. Branches that caught on them as she raced through the woods had torn her clothing. She needed several stitches for a gash in the back of her head that she'd received when Gil rammed her into the tree. But she scarcely noticed the pain that gripped her own body.

Every ounce of energy and attention she gave to Reid. She owed him her life, possibly that of her sister's. He couldn't die.

When he stirred, she stood up from her chair and went over to his bedside. His gaze swept around the room slowly, then focused unsteadily on her.

"How...how did I get here?" he asked, grimacing.

Susan explained briefly. "I'm sorry. If I hadn't been so stupid and gone with Gil, this wouldn't have happened."

"I'm a police officer. Things like this come with the territory." Reid reached out for her hand. "Are you okay?"

His touch was a strange, faltering gesture. Gripping onto his hand, Susan closed her eyes. After all that had taken place in the last several days, she wanted to touch, however briefly, something positive. "You saved my life," she told him.

A crooked smile spread over his battered face. "And you saved mine. So we're even."

"What happened to Markum?" Reid asked the next morning when Susan, accompanied by Harry, stopped by to see him in the intensive care unit where he was being kept for observation. Her car and Reid's patrol car had been brought back to Lake Center the night before by a couple of the men from the Rescue Squad. Through the partially open curtain across the room, Susan saw her sister's limp, still form lying between sterile the white sheets. Strands of her long, pale hair clung to the pillow-top.

"Gil didn't make it," Harry explained in response to Reid's question.

Reid was silent a moment. Although he was obviously in pain, he looked much better than he had the night before. His bruises had been cleaned and treated, and he wore a hospital gown. "Do you mind telling me once again what was going on out there, why Gil was chasing you?"

Susan explained how Gil had tricked her into taking him home, how he had admitted his part in Kim's 'accident.' With a shiver, she related how he had tried to strangle her to keep her from telling what he had done.

"If you hadn't come along when you did…" Susan shuddered at the thought. "How was it that you were in that area?"

"I suspected Gil was mixed up with Preston in some way." Reid spoke carefully, slowly, pausing to take a labored breath now and then. "Too many things leaned in that direction. Although Marisa rescinded her statement about Preston being at Gil's place, I suspected she was coerced into lying. If what she first stated was true, it put him and Preston together on the afternoon Preston was killed. I've been keeping an eye on Gil's movements. I was in the hospital parking lot when you and Gil left together. I tried to follow you, but lost you in traffic."

"I've had bad vibes a time or two while working on a case, but never as bad as I had when I saw you and Gil drive away from the hospital together. I had no idea where you'd gone." Reid paused, grimacing as he placed his hand on his rib cage. "I took the chance that you might be at Gil's place. When I arrived there and found no one home, I took the other way back, hoping I might meet you coming from that direction."

"Thank God!" Susan spoke softly but with profound gratitude.

After talking to Reid a few minutes longer, Susan and Harry moved over to Kim's bedside.

Harry had come to the hospital to get Susan the night before, after her injuries had been treated. Relief, then joy had spread across his wrinkled countenance when she told him what had happened, and that Kim hadn't killed Al Preston.

Now, as she peered down at her sister, Susan despaired how pale and deathlike Kim appeared. Was she to lose the sister she had known for such a short time? She bit down on her lip to hold back the fear rising inside her. Seized by the realization of how close to death she and Reid had come, how she, too, could be lying inert and lifeless, Susan felt a tremor slither through her slender frame. When she shivered, Harry reached out and placed his arm around her shoulder. Tears pooled in her eyes at his touch.

As, through the mist that blurred her eyes, she saw Kim move slightly, then began to stir, Susan's heart caught and her breath lodged in her throat.

Kim's lids fluttered open and she stared up at them, trying to focus her eyes. "Hi," she croaked in a harsh whisper.

Susan choked back the lump in her throat. "Hi yourself."

"Is this a wake, or am I still alive?" Kim asked in a feeble voice.

Susan flinched from the pain in her face as a smile curved her lips. "You're alive. How do you feel?"

Kim groaned. "I'm not sure." Frowning in concentration, she tried to focus her gaze on Susan's face. "What happened to you, or am I seeing in black and blue?"

Susan gave her sister a brief account of what had occurred the previous evening. "Reid's in a bed across the room," she explained.

"And Gil's dead?' Kim marveled in disbelief.

Susan nodded.

Kim's gaze lowered. "What goes around comes around," she said quietly, twisting the corner of the sheet in her fingers. Apparently seeing the irony of her statement, she added, "Looks like I got mine, too, doesn't it?" After another long, reflective pause, she said, "I can't believe that you actually shot at Gil."

"For all the good it did. But I had to do something."

"You almost fainted when I showed you the gun I had in my desk," Kim reminded Susan.

Susan's mouth curved wryly. "I didn't have time to faint last night. I was too busy trying to stay alive."

"I did my best to discourage you. To make you go back home, Susan, but you kept trying to *save* me. I promise I'll make it up to you—if I pulled through this...."

Susan took her sister's flaccid hand in her own, willing her strength and breath into Kim's battered body. "Of course you're going to make it."

For an instant, as she held her sister's hand, Susan was concerned she might hurt her. But intuitively, she knew her sister wouldn't notice the pain, that she needed love and forgiveness. Sitting on the edge of the bed, Susan stroked the back of Kim's hand.

Kim took a deep breath and exhaled it slowly. Her brown eyes were dark orbs in her pale face. "I got my pint of blood, didn't I? It's strange. I lived for this moment—to see Gil get his. I dreamed about it for so long, yet now that it's happened, I don't feel any satisfaction. I feel empty, burned out. I care about Kyle. I didn't want to hurt him. I know there can never be anything between us now. I hope, if he and

Marisa can see their way through this, they'll get back together. Hopefully, he can eventually forgive me. I know I'll never forgive myself."

"Don't be so hard on yourself," Susan said. "It's over now. Concentrate on getting well."

"Because of me two men are dead," Kim went on in a voice weighed with remorse. "Not very nice men, I'm sure we'll all agree, but human beings no less, and it makes me no less guilty. Neither Gil nor I could go on playing God forever, could we? I realize now that punishing him for his crimes, whatever they were, wasn't up to me. Too bad it took so long and the shedding of blood for me to come to that conclusion."

She paused to rest momentarily, then shook her head in disbelief. "How I could think that The Weasel and I could get away with the crazy scheme we'd concocted is something I'll never be able to figure out."

Susan gave her a small smile. She knew her sister had the resilience to bounce back. Kim had always been a fighter. A survivor. Susan saw that she, too, had always managed to make it in one way or another, although not without scars. Both of them had sought love, but had been unable to hold onto it. They were more alike, their lives more similar than they thought.

"I've been pretty hard on you, haven't I, Uncle Harry?" Kim said in a sober tone. "I guess I was jealous. I wanted all of Maggie's attention."

"Now, Kim, you don't have to..." Harry protested.

Ignoring his protest, Kim continued. "I thought my father didn't want me so I needed to prove, especially to myself, that someone did. I craved, needed Aunt Maggie's love all the more."

"Our father tried to get you back when he remarried," Susan pointed out. "But Maggie wouldn't let you go."

"I didn't know that. I've always thought he didn't want me, that he blamed me for my mother's death."

"I don't think that's true," Harry said. "But Susan's right. Maggie had grown so attached to you that she refused to give you up."

"I didn't know," Kim said again. "I've resented Susan all these years because our father kept her and not me."

"He didn't have much choice," Susan emphasized. "You were much better off with Maggie and Harry. If you and my step-mother had lived under the same roof, there wouldn't have been one on it." She gave her sister a weak smile.

Kim was silent for a moment, as if to absorb what she had learned. "Putting up with me must have been a blast for you, Harry. You should have put me over your knee and paddled me at least once a day."

"It wasn't because I didn't want to a time or two," Harry said. When Kim laughed, he added gruffly, "But I intend to do exactly that from now on if you give me grief."

Kim smiled at him, tears glistening in her eyes. After a brief silence, she spoke again. "When my doctor came in to see me this morning he said I'm better. I suppose you'll be leaving soon, Susan, going to California to see Mark."

"Mark?" Susan asked with a light laugh. "Who's Mark?" She hadn't thought about her ex-husband in days. "I'm going back to St. Paul in a day or two. I've decided to take the rest of my vacation when you get out of the hospital so I can be with you. I called the office, and it's okay. I'm sure you'll be here for a while yet. I'll come back on weekends to see you."

Kim's lips curved into a weak smile. "Maybe we'll have a chance to be real sisters yet. We can borrow each other's clothes and scrap like cats and dogs...."

"I'm looking forward to it." Susan blinked at the mist in her eyes. "But don't expect to win all the fights."

Kim chuckled softly. "My, my, who have we here?"

Two days later, as Susan was getting ready to go to the hospital to visit Kim and Reid again, the doorbell sounded.

When she opened the door, her mouth jaw dropped at the sight of Reid. "You're out of the hospital already?"

He grinned at her. "I don't know if it's because you can't keep a good man down, or if the nurses got tired of hearing me bellyache."

Susan laughed. Her gaze swept over him with both concern and admiration. There were still bruises and dark marks on his face where Gil had struck him. He was wearing an open-necked shirt and chinos that did nothing to diminish the aura of masculinity or the quiet strength he exuded in spite of his injuries.

"Surely you aren't going back to work right away," she said.

"I'm not quite up to that. I'm taking a week off."

"Are you sure you should be walking around like this?" Susan asked.

"The doctor taped my ribs and gave me some pain pills. It hurts like hell when I move wrong and I have a slight headache, but they couldn't find anything else wrong with me." Reid gave her a crooked grin. "At least, nothing that wasn't wrong with me before."

Smiling, Susan stepped aside and motioned for him to enter.

He walked stiffly, favoring his ribs. "I thought I'd stop by and see how you're feeling this morning."

"Compared to two days ago?"

"Since Kim's improving I suppose you'll be leaving for California soon," Reid ventured carefully.

"Now that I've survived the first ten days of my vacation?" Susan said with a wry laugh. "After talking to Mark on the phone, I realize things won't be any different than they were before. I don't intend to go back to being the old Susan. I want to make my own decisions, right or wrong. I'm going back to work in a day or so, but I'll return to see Kim as often as I can. When she gets out of the hospital, she'll be staying here with Harry for a while. I'm sure it will go better this time than when Kim was younger."

"So you'll be coming back to Lake Center from time to time?" Reid said.

"I'm sure you would rather I stay out of town, mind my own business and stay out of yours, right?"

Laugh lines crinkled at the corners of Reid's eyes. "I wouldn't mind a little interfering now and then."

Susan grinned at him. "Your injuries must be effecting your head."

Her gaze searched his face. The shadows had disappeared from his eyes, and there was warmth in his smile that had been absent before.

Her track record with men so far revealed that she wasn't a good judge of character. She had loved Mark, but it hadn't worked out. She didn't want to experience such pain and disappointment again. She had misjudged Gil, had been forewarned about him, but hadn't heeded. Deep down, she had known nothing would come of it.

She was going to think long and hard before becoming involved in another relationship.

"Maybe, if I'm elected sheriff this fall, you should put in your application for deputy." Reid spoke flippantly, his mouth curving upward at the corners. "We'd make a helleva team...provided you can handle it, of course."

Susan laughed. "After what I've been through the past week, nothing's going to effect me. But thanks for the offer. I'll take it into consideration."

"Take as long as you like. I'll be here." His eyes, when they met hers, said more than his words.

# # #

0-595-74644-6

Printed in the United States
1042900001B